Werewolf Vampire Witch

E.A. BUNDY

<u>OTHER BOOKS BY E.A. BUNDY:</u>

The Not-Witch
The Pigeon Catcher
Dark-Dreams Girl (prequel to *The Pigeon Catcher*)
Country Cousin in the Wild Woods
Wild Horse Girl (sequel to *Country Cousin*)
Phillip Marrow, Jr. The Private Eye
Henrietta H. House
Captain Dreade
Spider Wars

<u>ALSO PUBLISHED BY SINGING WINDS PRESS:</u>
Paul's Letters to the Nabateans by Mary Dulebohn
Old Man Gun by Wes Applegate

ACKNOWLEDGMENTS

A big THANK YOU to early readers who gave their feedback on parts of the manuscript, including: Noël, Marian, Andrea, Timothy and more recently Mary & the tireless efforts of Noelle and SWP.

DEDICATION

This story about the *Werewolf Vampire Witch* is dedicated to:
Savannah & Matthew

Werewolf
Vampire
Witch

E.A. Bundy

~Singing Winds Press~
Dallas, Oregon
Printed in the USA

BOOK ONE

WEREWOLF INDEPENDENCE

1: NIGHTMARE, PLEASE
—BEGINS *Before* Sadie Hawkins Dance—

*H*IS DARK FORM STALKED DOWNWIND of the small girl, and remained invisible to her in the shadows cast by the full moon. Why was she out there alone at night? It didn't matter. Blood lust was upon him, and she was his for the taking. His mouth watered simply from thinking about it.

Ahead, he saw her stumble in the deep gloom. She cried out. Unable to hold himself back any longer, he leapt forward across the uneven ground. Propelled by the powerful lure of her fear-flavored scent, his tongue wiped across his sharp fangs, anticipating the taste of her.

Drawing nearer, he slowed, crouched low, and then crept silently closer. She whimpered, but not because of him. She was lost...young and alone. Would he end it swiftly, killing her before she knew he was there?

Because of his exceptional night vision, her eyes glowed in her face as she sniffled. Her breath came in little gasps, and then halted. Did she sense him at last? A small hand reached out, not exactly toward him, but disturbingly close.

"Mommy." Her arm wavered uncertainly. "Is that you?"

Her body begged for devouring. Enough delay. His shaggy form rose to full height, and his bared teeth reflected in the pupils of her pathetic, unseeing eyes. A growl formed in the base of his throat.

She spoke a hesitant word, "Conall?"

Her voice was somehow familiar, and that single word was a haunting echo he nearly recognized. He sniffed her odor. Where had he smelled that scent before? The answer escaped him.

She stumbled forward, her tiny hand brushing his nostrils. Small fingers touched the hair of his muzzle. No prey had managed that before. Something in her touch brought an additional memory. He searched her face. Recognition came close, loomed nearer still—

Baying hounds drew his attention. They were on his trail, only moments away from discovering him. The troublesome dogs would interrupt his kill, ruining his delicious feast, and then destroy him.

No. He would not let them. Capture and death could be avoided if he left at once. There would be time for the little she-thing later.

He bounded into the night, wrapping shadows around him... but soon tired of the hounds' interference. The pack must pay. He circled around to the rear, picking out a straggler. The kill was quick, efficient, and with one enemy gone, he raced after the next...and then on to another.

The third hound turned when attacked, yelping even as his throat was seized. The remainder of the pack responded too rapidly, leaving no time to finish his third kill. The lanky wolf was faster than his pursuers, but they were masters of the scent trail and would not give up, tracking him tirelessly.

Did he have time to return for his kill?

No. The pack would harass him before he could savor her flesh. He ran for the stream. He would lead them in a desperate chase, and then double back to see how many he could kill before they caught on to his deadly repeating game.

*L*YING IN HIS BED IN INDEPENDENCE, Oregon, Conall wished for morning's arrival. He was sweat drenched, and his body ached as if from heavy exertion. He could not push the vivid images from his mind, and one in particular, his sister's face as her small hand reached out to him.

Turning on the light, his breath caught in his throat. Red stains soiled his sheets. His hands were bloody as well—but not from *his* blood. He looked in the mirror. Vile redness ringed his mouth.

Repulsed, he wiped frantically with an unstained portion of the sheet. Not again—another nightmare? Unfortunately, even bad dreams did not leave real blood behind. What was it then? He shuddered with fear. Was his sister okay?

In the bathroom, he cleaned his face and hands before he moved on and peeked into her room, checking her bed to be certain she was safe. Yes, she was there, sleeping peacefully.

What a relief. Returning to his bedroom, he stripped away the stained sheets. Eventually, wrapped in just a blanket, merciful sleep claimed him again at last.

*I*N THE MORNING, CONALL LOOKED in the mirror just to be certain he had thoroughly cleaned his face from all telltale traces of the night before. Satisfied, he studied his appearance. Falsely, he seemed to be a typical seventeen-year-old boy, tall and lean, with a dark complexion. His almost black hair tended to fall across his dark eyes. He pushed it back until he was satisfied there were no red mark betrayals. Not a single clue of his terrible affliction showed.

Looks, however, could be deceiving. Despite a tiny grin that occasionally appeared on his thin face, Conall mostly hid his smile from the world because of terrifying visions—or were they memories? Whatever they were, those images haunted him. He left the bathroom and went to find something to eat.

A message addressed to Conall rested on the kitchen table. It was in his mother's handwriting, but the words were larger than usual, for emphasis. Parts were even underlined, and if she had actually stood there, she'd be yelling at him.

The meaning of the note came in two simple questions. "What was all that crashing around in your bedroom?" And "Why did you play those recorded howling sounds in the middle of the night?"

Conall didn't know the answers to her questions. He could guess, but he didn't want to. The Smartphone rang in his pocket, and he struggled to get it out and check the caller I.D. Not his mother. Big relief. It was his best friend—not really his girlfriend.

"Hi, Sadey."

"Conall," she said, "guess what."

He voiced the first thing that came to mind, thankful for the diversion. "Your hamster escaped again, and you need me to help catch it."

"No. This is serious." Her voice took on a mature tone. "You know there's a big dance coming up next month, right?"

Dancing was really not his thing. "I guess so."

"Are you going?"

He knew the reason for her question, but said, "I'm not sure, why?" He liked this part. It would keep her on the defensive, and prevent him from thinking about scarier, more personal things. Conall knew very well it was a Sadie Hawkins dance, a variation of her name—and it only made sense she would ask him.

"I was just curious if you are going," she said. There was a disconcertingly long pause. "Are you still there, Conall?"

"Yes." He smiled. Now she would learn how difficult it was for boys sometimes, and especially for him.

"What are you doing?" she asked.

He glanced at the note. "Reading," he said, which was part-true.

"Oh. I didn't mean to disturb you."

"That's okay, but I guess I should get back to my reading...unless there is something you wanted to ask me." He briefly smothered his lips in the crook of his arm so he would not laugh out loud.

A moment later, he raised his Smartphone back up, and asked, "What did you say?" All the while knowing that if she had any idea he was playing with her, she would get even.

"I just asked, do you want to come over and watch one of the *Iron Man* movies with me? Or, you could bring *The Spirit,* or one of your *Blade* flicks...."

She knew he was a sucker for pretty much any of the movies based on comic books. Plus, her family had the biggest flat screen TV available, and he loved watching movies on their set.

She added, "You can bring *Avatar* if you like."

That was his top choice, right up there with *Blade Runner.* Those two films he ranked maybe even higher than superhero flicks. Plus, going over to her place would get him out of his house. If his mom was still mad when she got back, he would be gone.

"Okay," he said. "I'll bring several along, and you can pick one."

"Cool. See you soon." She ended the call before he could respond further.

The other good news about visiting Sadey was he doubted she had the guts to ask him to the dance in person. She was more likely to use e-mail, texting, or her friend, Amber. His real problem had nothing to do with Sadey. His dilemma resulted from the day on which the dance would occur, near the next full moon. It was a dangerous time for Conall, and he always seemed to black out on those evenings.

In his bedroom, he sorted through his movies for ones he knew that Sadey liked as well, and paused at *Airplane.* Smiling, he remembered how hard she'd laughed at certain parts. Conall knew that if he didn't go to the dance with her, she would find someone else—a scary thought.

With his selections in his backpack, he went out to the garage to get his motor scooter, and sped off. The wind whistled past him and seemed to draw his troubles away. When he arrived at Sadey's, she ushered him speedily into her family room, which was all arranged for the occasion. They seated themselves in the two lounge chairs that she'd positioned at the perfect viewing distance. Once seated, they were spaced comfortably apart, and strategically between them she had situated both of their favorite soft drinks, plus a large bag of popcorn.

One of the things that made watching movies at her house so great was the awesome surround-sound system. As Conall and Sadey became more comfortable for the show, he did something impulsive, and said, "I don't know if I'm going to the dance, or not."

"Me, neither," she added, tipping her head forward thoughtfully. "I feel a lot of pressure to ask a guy, but I'm scared to call anyone."

Conall felt guilty for messing with her. "Yeah," he said, "asking someone out is hard."

"It's more than that for me," she replied. "A lot more."

The silence between them turned awkward. So uncomfortable, he found himself saying, "Did you want me to go with you?"

What was he doing? He couldn't attend the dance. What if he did, and something awful happened?

"I'd hoped to ask you out," she said, "but I know you don't like to boogie. I thought we could just go there together, if that's okay. We wouldn't actually have to dance."

His guilt piled up higher.

"There is something else," she said.

He waited for her to continue, and after staring at the floor for a long time she finally said, "I never told anyone about this, but when I get nervous, bad things happen."

Conall could relate to that, and prompted her, "Such as...?"

She whispered, "Well...I think I'm a witch."

Conall laughed. "Why do you believe that?" She was totally *not* witch-like. There was nothing witcherly about her in the least.

"When I put things in the microwave, they cook instantly."

He said, "That's what microwaves are all about."

"*Before* I push the Start button."

Not feasible, he thought, it must be a shorted-out switch that starts when the door bangs shut. He asked, "Are you certain?"

"Yes, and if I just think about putting my hair into a ponytail...."

Conall stared. Sadey's hair had instantly, all by itself, formed into a ponytail. Where had the tie-band come from? What he'd just seen was definitely impossible. He stammered, "Uh...."

"That's not all," she said rapidly, "the more I worry about things I don't want to happen, the more likely they are to occur. Did you hear about the time in science class when—"

"You showed up in your bikini," he finished for her, barely controlling a laugh because it was a sensitive issue for Sadey.

"But I didn't wear it to class," she explained. "It was the middle of winter, and I was bored, sitting there daydreaming about being on the beach in Hawaii. All of a sudden, the whole room was silent. Mr. Seare cleared his throat, and when I looked down, I was in this skimpy little floral bikini." She turned red just telling about it. "My worst fear is...what if I daydream of myself in a hot bath? I had a hard time explaining about the bikini, how could I possibly justify being bare-naked in class?"

"I'm not sure, but If you do," Conall said, "make it during fourth period so I don't miss out." He thought he was being humorous.

She leaned over faster than he'd imagined possible and hit him on the shoulder, really hard. She screeched, "It's not funny!" Then stood up and raced from the room, grumbling, "Guys are so stupid—but what did I expect?"

Conall felt extremely awkward sitting alone in Sadey's family room in front of the blank TV screen, so he munched on popcorn. She eventually returned, but so quietly that he scarcely noticed when she sat down. He peeked over at her, trying not to let her see that's what he was doing, and found she had been crying.

Ashamed for his contribution to her hurt feelings, Conall knew he must apologize. The problem was, he had a mouth full of popcorn. If he could just clear it, he might be able to speak. In desperation, he swallowed a too-large amount, and felt sharp edges grind their way down his throat. He coughed, and little particles went everywhere.

It was her turn to laugh. "Serves you right."

"I'm sorry," he whispered, choking down the last remnants. "I didn't mean to hurt your feelings." A partial husk clung to the back of his tongue. He tried to clear it, but was forced to use his finger, and even then he encountered extreme difficulty.

Sadey had a great laugh at his expense. It went on and on until he chuckled as well. When they caught their breaths, Conall tried to explain. "It's just so hard to imagine you being a witch. You don't look like one. Don't witches have black hair? Yours is light, summer blonde—and you aren't ugly...." He couldn't bring himself to say she was really pretty, although she was. "You almost never wear black."

"I do in my dreams," she said, "and in many of them I wear a tall, pointed, black witch's hat, as well."

"You certainly don't act like a witch," he said.

Sadey changed the subject. "Do you remember in Tall Mage Middle School when Miss Hunkley grew a mustache during class?"

He recalled it vividly. Letting his body settle back into place, he remembered that time when Sadey was in sixth grade. He'd been in eighth, but everybody in all the grades knew about the incident.

"Miss Hunkley said something mean to me," Sadey recounted, "and I got angry at her. She eventually talked about math, or whatever, but I was still upset, and started daydreaming, picturing her with a mustache. I didn't really want her to grow one, but when I looked up at her, there it was.

"The whole class stared at our teacher. When she asked what was wrong, one of her new facial hairs tickled her nose, and she sneezed real loud. Putting her hand to her mouth, she felt the mat of her mustache, screamed, and ran from the room."

Conall added, "I heard she had plastic surgery to get rid of it." He was relieved to be talking about Sadey instead of himself, but surely she didn't believe she had caused the mustache.

"Laser surgery," she corrected, "and my teacher took early retirement the next year. When I get mad at my friend Amber, I worry she'll end up looking like Miss Hunkley. No matter how hard I tried, I couldn't make our teacher's facial hair disappear. It seems like only bad things come from my magic, and I can't control it."

"You made your hair go into a ponytail," he reminded her, trying to be encouraging. At the same time, he realized she really had done that. He'd seen the astonishing event himself. Could she have caused the teacher's mustache?

"The ponytail happens if I just think about it, and often, it's during a class. Amber has asked me—I don't know how many times—'When did you put that in?'

"But I can't magically take a ponytail out."

The moment Sadey mentioned that final apparent truth to Conall, her hair-tie appeared in her hand, and the ponytail fell away into her normal hairdo. She reached up, feeling the shape of it to be certain, and said, "That's a first."

He stared, knowing his mouth was open. How had she managed to do that?

"The thing is..." he paused, "like I said at first, you aren't the only one with a problem."

He wanted to tell her about his dark secret, but fear prevented him. Anyway, there wasn't real proof, except for the red sheets, that he was actually a—he dared not think the dreaded word.

"Who has anything like this to worry about besides me?" she asked. "I didn't want to believe," her voice paused. "I don't think Santa Claus is real, or the tooth fairy, or the Easter bunny."

As she talked, Conall thought her "problem" was minor in comparison to his. She was into instant cooking, and fashion makeovers, not life and death. "Maybe you're starting to get more control of it," he said, thinking about her ponytail.

"You don't believe me, do you?"

"Actually, I do—but about the dance," he said, purposely changing the subject. "I'm not sure I'll be here that day, but if I am, I'll be happy to go with you."

Sadey flung herself across the distance between them and hugged Conall, and then withdrew self-consciously. "Thanks. You're the only guy I wanted to go with."

Her statement reassured him. Feeling happy inside, he said, "Maybe you want to just relax, and daydream right now—about a hot bath, perhaps?"

Rather than getting angry, she smiled and said, "I'm imagining *you* in a hot bath, and I'm going to make *your* clothes disappear."

Could she really do that? Conall swallowed with difficulty because all of a sudden he felt unaccountably warm.

2: DANCING?

CONALL PACED THE FLOOR OF his bedroom. Where had the time gone? In only two days the dreaded Friday would arrive. He had tried relaxation tapes without success. They'd worked in the past, but not lately. His anxiety grew as the Sadie Hawkins dance neared.

He wanted to go and support his friend, but it was still a couple days away, and he was more jittery than usual when entering that dangerous part of the month. When he'd finally looked on his calendar, the full moon turned out to be exactly the same night as the school dance, which was one of the biggest events at Centrist High. If he went, and anyone made him mad, or he became too tense, or maybe just for no apparent reason at all—

He refused to let himself think about all of that. Each time Conall contemplated attending the Sadie Hawkins event, images of mauled corpses filled his mind. Where the visions came from, he wasn't certain. Hopefully, they weren't flashbacks. Sometimes, there was enough flesh left on a gnawed face in his vision that he could identify the victim.

Too often, the corpse's image turned out to be that of his little sister. He cringed just thinking about it. Nights seemed to be a mixture of terrible dreams, and reality, but how to tell them apart? His biggest fear was of awakening one morning to discover his sister's mauled body.

The phone rang and he answered, not recognizing the number.

"Conall?" a familiar young female voice asked.

"Hi, Sis." His hand shook. Surely, it was just a coincidence, her calling when he had pictured her dead.

"We're at the mall. Mom says for you to stay home. She wants to talk when we get back." Emily made a sound Conall knew meant she was sticking her tongue out at him, and then she hung up. His mother often had his sister call him from random phones so he wouldn't know who it was, and consequently, he'd answer.

Conall struggled to picture positive things because so close to the full moon many events could trigger—he mustn't think about it.

He chose to focus instead on an imaginary time when he and Sadey might ride in a car together. He pictured the dance night, and them traveling from their homes at the edge of Independence, to Centrist high school, which also served the adjoining town of Monmouth. In his fantasy, Conall had on his sports coat. No way was he going to wear his entire suit. Sadey had on a formal dress, and a tiara held her hair on top of her head.

In the next moment of his fantasy, she was nude, having accidentally pictured herself in a hot bath. Conall smiled at that part of his mental movie, until he saw her probable reaction, and then he felt guilty. He was not going to the dance anyway, and besides, *his* daydreams *never* came true.

Sometimes, after Conall thought of Sadey naked, he punished himself by remembering his dreaded disorder. Occasionally, like this morning, he had spotted red traces around his mouth, and scrubbed them off ferociously.

The noisy rampage of the little mutt next door interrupted Conall's thoughts. Dogs disliked him. Actually, they hated him, and the neighbor's little pet was no exception. The feeling was mutual, and Conall went to close his second story window to shut out the sound. In the course of that action, he looked down at the toy poodle yapping noisily from the adjoining yard.

Conall flung the window shut, and the little dog looked up. When their eyes locked, the small creature stopped barking, and raced for its house with fright.

The phone rang in Conall's pocket, broadcasting music through his room. This time, he looked to see who it was—Amber. What did *she* want? He said, "Hello."

"Conall, did Sadey really ask you to the dance? She says she did. But she's such a wimp, I don't believe her."

"Yes." He said, thinking she'd kind of asked in a roundabout way. At least, they had reached a mutual understanding—but only *if* he went.

"Really?" said Amber. "Amazing. I got to go, bye."

Conall looked down at his phone. Thank goodness his mother had not taken it away as she'd threatened. It rang while he was absently looking at the little LCD screen, and he nearly dropped the thing. Not registering the fact her picture was absent, and assuming it was Amber again, he said, "Yeah?"

"Uh..." there was a pause on the other end. The male voice said hesitantly, "Is this Conall L. Canis?"

Oh great, Conall thought, a school administrator. Nobody else used his full name. The L. stood for Lupis, not to be mistaken for lupus: the disease. He was preparing himself to say, "Sorry, no. You got the wrong guy," and hang up, except for what he heard next.

"This is James Joyce," the man said. "Not *the* James Joyce, I just have the same name. My folks had a sense of humor, I guess. Anyway, the reason I called...."

Who was *the* James Joyce? Conall wondered.

"I need an illustrator for a comic book I'm developing. I've finished the story, but I need someone who can draw. Besides penciling, you would do the inking, coloring, and even the lettering. I saw your illustration in an annual that was put out by the *Horse of Darkness Comics Press*. Those guys are great, aren't they?"

Conall was stunned. Somebody wanted *him* to illustrate a comic book? This had to be a gag. Except, none of his family or friends knew he created comics. Not even his bratty little sister. Therefore, it must be for real. He stammered, "Uh...."

"Think it over," said the man. "I will send you the first ten pages of text by e-mail—or maybe I'll send the whole thing. Read at least the start of it so you have a better idea what I'm creating. Most everybody is into vampires now, but I'm making this comic about werewolves." The man howled like a wolf.

Conall was petrified. What did the guy know about him? As the call abruptly ended, Conall sat there on his bed with a million questions running through his mind. The phone rang and he answered, again without identifying the caller. He assumed it was the Joyce fellow, and not knowing what he would say to the man, he simply mumbled, "Hello."

Sadey's voice sounded surprised. "Conall? Is that you?"

"Who did you expect to answer *my* phone, Sadey, the boogeyman? What do you want?" He cringed inside for taking out his mood on her.

"Oh.... Well, it didn't sound like you. I just need to talk about something—important."

"Could it wait until tomorrow?" he asked. "I just got off the phone, and it was a really important conversation. I think the guy is going to call me back. Maybe you and I can talk at school; won't that work?"

She hurriedly asked, "Did Amber phone you?"

"Yes, just a minute ago."

"Well, you know what a rumor mill she is. Amber is telling everyone you and I will attend the dance, *together*. She says we are now *'going out,'* as in...."

"I get it," he said. "I still don't know for sure if I can make it. If I can, it'll be with you, like we talked about."

"I know," she answered, "its just that Amber...is such a gossip. So the next thing we'll probably hear is that you and I are sleeping together."

"Uh..." Conall had not seen that coming. The image flashed through his mind of Sadey naked in the car on the way to the dance. "I will try to go with you. I really will." Then he added, "Don't worry about Amber. I need to hang up for now, though, because I think that guy is going to call me right back."

He ended the conversation. Too much was happening all at once, causing Conall's breathing to accelerate, and his pulse was pounding. He knew all too well what the Hulk must go through. Conall, however, had at least four things that tended to trigger his "defect," instead of mostly one. There was the full moon, of course, plus rage, fear, and even sexy images—any of those could do it.

Problematically, at that very moment he was experiencing three out of the four. Obviously, there was only one more day until the moon reached full size, so he was in the critical zone for that. Sadey had triggered his sexual thoughts, and he was *afraid* of going to the dance. In the middle of all that, this guy James Joyce wanted him to draw werewolves. Thinking of werewolves also brought out his anger, and that made all four of the elements that could trigger....

Conall felt the prickling sensations all over his body and knew the next stage was rapidly approaching—hairs would pop out everywhere. After that, he would lose consciousness. There was always the fear he might hurt someone he cared for, like his little sister, or Sadey, maybe even his mother.

The worst part was the not knowing about what actually occurred during such episodes. Did he truly transform, and if so, what did he become? He was pretty sure he knew. He feared the pictures his mind conjured up about what he did when he blanked out. Currently, that imagery was about him and Sadey alone in a car on the night of a full moon. What would really happen if she were naked? Conall swallowed hard because he *knew* what would happen. He'd convert to his other form. Even if he didn't kill Sadey—a really big if—she would see him as a hairy monster.

If he did not ravage her in his animal form—a truly disgusting thought—she would certainly be repulsed. Their friendship would end, along with his social standing, if not his total existence at school, and that was only if she survived.

Were his hairs already growing? Conall thought so. If he didn't stop what was happening, it would be too late. His phone single-chimed, meaning he probably had a new e-mail. Using the touch screen, he accessed the Internet icon. There were three new messages. One was from James Joyce. Conall opened it, and read:

Conall Canis, Please consider my offer. I need an illustrator with your style. Your work is unique, and I want it for my comic. See attached storyline. Let me know what you think. Thanks in advance—
James

There was a large paper-clipped file included. Conall feared to look at it. Besides, how had some random guy gotten a hold of his cell phone number and his email account information? Conall couldn't deal with that at the moment. He must calm down first, and the email about a werewolf comic book was not helping.

Why had James Joyce selected Conall to illustrate it? Agitated, Conall paced the floor of his room. Did this Joyce guy know something about Conall aside from the fact he could draw?

While pacing, Conall felt the small hairs on the back of his neck prickling. They were definitely starting to grow. He growled low in the back of his throat. It was long past time to take a chill pill and calm down. If he didn't do something quickly, the transformation would happen earlier than usual. It wouldn't wait for the night of the full moon.

Conall raced down the hall to the bathroom and splashed cold water in his face. That didn't help. He ran some warm water and filled the washbasin. Dunking his head under the surface, he let the warmth seep into his skin. A peaceful feeling slowly engulfed his body. The warm water was working. Maybe a hot bath would be the needed tonic, so he began filling up the tub.

He remembered a wolf at the Oregon Zoo in Portland. It

seemed to have only two behaviors—lying about, or pacing around the fenced-in area. Conall felt like walking the floor, too. Instead, he made himself take a bath. Lying in the liquid warmth, peace slowly filled him.

The soothing water worked so well that after a time Conall thought about the drawing proposal from James Joyce without getting tense. Conall's secret desire was to be a comic book illustrator, and if the offer were real, this could be his big chance.

"Okay," he whispered, "Let's get a look at this guy's werewolf story."

Conall located his Smartphone in his pants pocket, where his jeans lay on the floor. Straightening with great care, to keep from dropping it in the water, he re-checked his e-mails.

The attachment from James Joyce was a thirty-page-long PDF. Conall began reading, but on the small screen it would take forever to finish. It seemed to be better-written than most comics. How many drawings could Conall turn out in three days? There might be enough time to rough out a few pages worth of panels. That would be ample results to let the guy decide if he still wanted Conall for his illustrator. Could Conall complete all the artwork for an entire comic? He had done short ones before, but just for fun, and definitely nothing so large. He paused. What was he doing? Only moments ago he'd nearly triggered shapeshifting, and it would take very little to do so in the present. But his desire to become a comic book illustrator was now overriding his fear.

He typed an e-mail reply to let James Joyce know there would be sample pages in a few days. Then he felt excited by the possibility the offer could mean for him. He left the bath, toweled off, pulled on his pants, and returned to his bedroom.

Conall began some preliminary thumbnail sketches. He had no idea, however, what to put for a cover drawing, but that could wait. He knew he wanted to place a large central panel on the first page. He would surround it with smaller ones to fill out the rest of that area. The main action would hit the reader right in the face. The background information would come from the supporting drawings around the outer edges of the page.

The rough thumbnail sketches would give ideas for the details needed in each final drawing. Conall worked intensely, dashing off several thumbnails. He knew the central panel on page one would be of a man changing into a werewolf. He put off doing that one, leaving the middle panel blank for the time being. Conall could not risk focusing on the transformation—the actual conversion from man to werewolf, which might trigger his untimely turning.

There would be more shapeshifting illustrations later in the comic. He could tell that from the attachment James Joyce had sent him. But if Conall could not do any of those, he might as well give up and tell the man to find somebody else.

Conall needed reference photos, and an idea came. What if he made video footage of a real shapeshifter—after all, he had a digital camcorder. If he hooked that to his MacBook, it would give him more memory to play with. He could adjust the resolution to just above web quality. Not high enough to eat-up all the available memory, since it might have to record for who knew how long?

With no more planning than that, he set up his camera in a corner where it would remain undisturbed. There was another benefit to this idea. He would finally know what happened when he blacked out. He was excited, but also scared of that possibility.

With such a video record, he could watch the body transformation—assuming there was one—as often as necessary to give details for his illustrations. So pleased was he by the new opportunity, he wanted to call Sadey and let her know. Not yet. She was unaware of his comic book illustrator dreams, or the condition he struggled with at each full moon. Maybe he would share those details with her afterward.

Conall sometimes wondered why no one had put together the facts. He usually missed a couple of days from school each month, and always at the full moon. He was super sensitive to that lunar phase, even when the weather was rainy and overcast for weeks at a time, and the moon was virtually invisible even when full. But most people did not keep track of such an event.

Initial excitement became nervousness. Conall left his drawing table and began pacing the floor. What was he thinking of? The whole idea was crazy.

A previous concern began to nag at him. He paced faster. Did this Joyce-guy know something about Conall besides the fact he could draw? There were better illustrations in that annual issue than his. Why had Conall been chosen above those?

The prickly sensation returned. One thing became clear. Conall could not possibly attend the dance with Sadey. It was far too dangerous. He had to let her know because she only had two days to find someone to replace him. He pulled out his phone and touched her number in his contacts.

"Sadey?" he stammered.

"Who did you expect to be answering *my* phone, Conall?"

He ignored her return barb. "I had to let you know that I'm sorry, but something has come up and I definitely can't go to the dance on Friday."

There was silence on the other end, and the quiet was too much for Conall. He continued by making things up as he went along. "Do you remember that important call I had?"

"Yes."

"Well, it turns out my Uncle Ralph, up in Portland...I've told you about him before. His wife is sick. She's in the hospital, and they need me to babysit my nephew."

Conall didn't even have a nephew, and his uncle wasn't married, but once the lying began, Conall kept right on going. "I'll be away for the next couple of days. Probably the weekend, or longer."

"I'm sorry about your aunt," Sadey said. "Hope it's not serious."

"I don't know what is wrong with her," said Conall, unable to decide on a fictitious disease. "Uncle Ralph didn't say, but I want you to know, except for this occurrence, I would go to the dance with you. I was even planning to dress up."

"Okay," said Sadey. "I better call Amber and tell her to update her rumor mill."

Conall thought Sadey sounded nervous—yet relieved.

"I'm not sure I'll go to the dance, either," she said just before she told him good-bye and hung up.

He breathed deeply. Staying home for the next couple of days was the safe thing to do—the smart thing. Poor Sadey, though, he was letting her down.

The sound of familiar vintage rock and roll music interrupted his thoughts. His phone was ringing again. Conall thought the number looked familiar.

"Did you read it yet?" It was James Joyce.

"Not all. I just got the e-mail."

"Well, read it and call me back." The guy hung up before Conall could say anything more.

3: BLACKOUT

WHEN CONALL AWOKE SOMETIME EARLY on Saturday morning, he felt awful, although that wasn't an unusual feeling to have after a full moon. His previous few days were a blur—at least for that moment. Nevertheless, he made himself get up and check his video on the laptop. He soon accessed the video's beginning, watching his body lying asleep in bed, but he stopped there. He couldn't force himself to proceed to where the most revealing footage would be located.

His phone rang on his nightstand exactly where he'd hastily placed it—like he always did—somewhere safe during the approach of a full moon. Of course, he had to do that before he reached the critical stage, for fear he might lose, or destroy it. Still not fully awake, he answered it to silence the loud music. The picture of Sadey was on the screen along with a missed call message. He hit the speaker.

"Hello," he said, his voice sounding groggy even to himself.

"Conall!" Sadey screamed. "You won't believe what happened. I wish you had been there. I've tried calling you half the night."

He mumbled, "I just woke up."

"I went to the dance after all, with Amber. At first, that new kid, Des, asked me to dance, and then he asked Amber. They were out on the gym floor, just starting to boogie, when everything stopped."

"What do you mean?" Conall asked, but he felt angry because the new kid had made a move on Sadey.

She raced on in her narrative, "The Deejay paused the music, and all the kids separated. At first, I couldn't see why. Then this big dog walked through the crowd. Only, it wasn't a dog. It was a wolf.

Amber screamed at it, and the thing leaped toward her.

"Des—you know him—that new kid. Well, he hid *behind* Amber. I thought sure the wolf would kill her."

Conall asked, "Are you certain it was a wolf?"

"Yes, and I screamed when I thought it was going to slaughter Amber. That is when it came for *me*. It bounded to just six feet away, maybe even less. There it stopped and stared into my eyes. I thought I was dead for sure. Then, *I* screamed, again.

"It turned away, and left after a moment, but I don't understand why. Nobody knows where the wolf went. I was so scared, I didn't even think about using my magi—" She cut her word off.

Conall carried his phone over to his laptop, and started searching through the video. Surely, it was just a coincidence that a large "dog" crashed the school dance on the night of a full moon.

"I wish you had been there," Sadey said. "Oh, I almost forgot. Some of the kids took pictures with their cell phones. Amber forwarded three photos to me. I e-mailed you a copy of the best one."

Conall let his Smartphone sink down to his side. Would the "wolf" have killed his best friend? Sadey's voice said something he did not hear accurately, so Conall raised his phone back up. Had she stated what he thought? He said, "Sorry, I didn't catch that last part."

"I want to know what you believe. Mr. Seare the biology teacher says there are no such things as wolves in this part of Oregon. You are smart. Look and see what *you* think—I'm waiting."

Reluctantly, Conall accessed his e-mails. The newest one from Sadey was already there. He noticed another message from James Joyce, but bypassed it.

Opening Sadey's message, Conall clicked on the attachment. It took a while to load. Could that thing in the picture be him?

So far, Conall hadn't the nerve to check his videocam footage.

"It does sort of look like a wolf," he told her. "It is hard to tell in that light...and he's moving. Plus, it's just a tiny image on my phone."

"There is supposed to be a better photo," she said. "It was taken with one of the newest phones at higher resolution. When I get a copy, I'll send it your way. Oh, how is your aunt?"

Conall forgot for a moment what Sadey was referring to. Then he remembered, and said hastily, "She is out of the hospital, and doing better." He hated lying, but there was no other choice. Unless, of course, he finally confessed that maybe the picture of the wolf was him—and then revealed to her that he had a defect more revolting than being a witch. Instead, he continued his awful lying.

"Good," said Sadey, "I'm glad to hear she's okay. I have to go. Amber is trying to get through, and maybe she got a clearer picture, now. You know how resourceful she is. She will certainly share with us, and I'll send it as soon as it arrives. See you—"

"Bye," he mumbled.

He forced himself to search through a good portion of the video to the footage he sought. He continued farther toward the beginning, afraid to stop and examine the hairy shape because he was so scared of the truth. The image was obviously a canine shape. He paused the video well beyond there, at the place where he had simply walked around in human form.

Conall looked at the frozen frame for a minute. He finally got the nerve to press play, and the video showed him walking feverishly, circling his bedroom. It reminded him of the wolf at the zoo. Only, he was still human at that point. Then his video self sped up its pacing.

Becoming fascinated, Conall wondered how fast he would eventually go. Pretty darned fast, he soon learned. It was like some of those speed walkers with exaggerated arm motions. In the video, unbelievably, he threw off his clothes. He watched himself run naked around the room. He'd even leapt over the bed, and jumped off the top of the dresser.

Eventually, the naked form on the screen crashed to the floor, and apparently dropped into a troubled sleep. Chills ran down the back of Conall's neck. He watched the video, in awe of the stark changes that had occurred in his body on Friday night. Hairs grew out of seemingly every pore. His narrow face elongated into a carnivorous muzzle with large canine teeth. His limbs morphed into four, equal-length wolf's legs. Most amazingly, a tail sprouted, and became full-sized in a few minutes.

The wolf's head rose from the floor. There was no hint of Conall remaining in those fierce eyes. The creature jumped to its feet and paced for a minute, and then it stopped in front of the bedroom window. Conall's room was on the second story. He watched in disbelief as the wolf's snout slid his bedroom window open by pushing the slider to the side. A moment later it bounded lightly through the gap—plunging out of sight into the darkness below.

Conall sat in shock. He let the scene of his empty room play uneventfully for several minutes. Then he rewound to the wolf lying on the floor during an inactive moment, and paused the video.

Checking his iPhone again, sure enough, there was a recent attachment from Sadey. Conall compared the two images—the new and clearer view of the wolf at the dance—in relation to his still form on the bedroom floor Friday night. They were definitely a match. Conall *had* gone to the dance after all.

Now what?

Conall went downstairs to find something to eat. He always got hungry when he was nervous. There was only one thing for him to do. He needed help. His dangerous problem could not wait any longer. Where could he get assistance, though?

A couple of times he had done Online research, and discovered a mental illness termed lycanthropy, or Werewolf Syndrome. Some of those afflicted became murderers. There were also cases of people with hair all over their faces, and upper bodies, but a Canadian researcher had determined they possessed a mutant gene.

Some *temporary* physical change had occurred within Conall. It was more than if he was simply going crazy. He had evidence, including pictures, plus the witnesses at the dance. Proof that his was an actual body transformation. He even had the video for complete confirmation.

Unless, of course, he was actually so insane that he had simply hallucinated the pictures, plus the film clip. No. Sadey had called and told him about the dance, the wolf, and the pictures. Surely, he could not simply have imagined all of that. But Conall decided he needed an independent observer just to be certain.

The only one he trusted enough to disclose his secret to was Sadey. Still, what would her reaction be? His story would make him sound nuts. Alternatively, if he did nothing, he could wake up some morning with the blood spatters of someone he loved on his face, only to later learn that a "rabid wolf" had killed a friend of his, or a close relative. He was startled to realize that he'd just left the kitchen after ravenously eating numerous items he barely registered, and he still had a handful of junk food.

He paced through his house. The rest of his family always slept in on Sundays. Could he awaken some morning to find his closest loved-ones mauled to death? He shuddered with the thought. His little sister could be a pain, but she was also sweet. She thought the world of Conall when she wasn't pestering him. Sometimes, he did not get along with his parents, either, but that never lasted very long.

Conall raced back to his room. He had left his phone on his desk. What if Sadey had called? He checked. She had not left a message. There was another e-mail from James Joyce. That was two Conall had not answered. Feeling guilty, he opened the first one.

Conall, how is the artwork coming? I have found a comic book press interested in publishing this. They say there is lots of interest about werewolves right now. They have two illustrators, and either of them can get right on it. I do not want to pressure you, but things are moving fast here. Let me know how the illustrations are going.
Cheers, James

Opening the second e-mail, Conall saw a briefer message.

Conall, if I don't hear from you by noon, I will have to find someone else. No hard feelings—James Joyce

Conall checked his watch. He could achieve little in the time remaining before the deadline, having completed nothing since the roughly-sketched thumbnails. Other issues now pressed in on him. He wrote a quick reply, including an apology. He simply said James Joyce should choose one of the other illustrators.

Then he dialed Sadey. Her phone began ringing. What was he going to say to her? Perhaps he'd start with, "I know you think we are friends." Then add, "I guess you believe you know everything about me. However, I forgot to share a small detail...."

Conall almost hung up. His finger poised above the *end* command to cancel his call. How much chance was there Sadey would believe what he told her, anyway? And even if she did not freak out—then what? Would she want to go to the police? Perhaps she would have him committed in a mental hospital. His finger lowered to end his call.

Then an awful image popped into his mind, of Sadey lying dead. He had been through all this before. There had to be a way to get help. He must take the chance. His finger lifted a safer distance above the phone.

A second image came into his mind. Conall imagined he was in a psychiatric ward undergoing shock treatment. His body jumped on the table, though he was securely strapped to it.

His phone vibrated and rang at the same time. That sensation, coupled with the image in his mind of electroshock, meant he nearly flipped it across the room. Heavy metal music pounded.

"Hello," Sadey said, as he connected to her call.

Conall responded immediately. "I have to see you—*now*."

Two minutes later, he sat on his motor scooter. His laptop was safely stored in his backpack and slung over his shoulders. He started the engine and put the gearshift into first. He would get to Sadey's in record time—

Conall rang the bell at her house. Where was she? Why was she taking so long? He tried the knob. It was unlocked. He entered, finally remembering to remove his safety helmet.

Sadey came down the hallway from her kitchen with a yogurt cup in her hand. "Conall? Uh, come on in. Oh...I guess you are in."

She laughed ironically.

Up in her bedroom, Conall paced around, talking non-stop. If he did not tell her everything, he would chicken out. She just sat there on her bed. At times, her mouth dropped open. Mostly, he did not watch her face—afraid of her reaction. He heard himself say, "wolf" several times, and finally, *werewolf*. She just stared. What did she think?

Conall went over to her dresser where he had placed his computer notebook. He started playing the video of him in his bedroom. His behavior in the video was just the way he had been acting since they got upstairs—rapid pacing.

Sadey moved closer to view the film.

He glanced at her face when the footage came to the part where he tore his clothes off. Her interest seemed to grow stronger, even as he became more self-conscious.

"Conall," she asked, "are you thinking of making X-rated films? I'm not sure I want to...this could be embarrassing." She laughed nervously. "Or really interesting." She started to look away, but then "forced" herself to notice each detail in the video.

Conall hoped she was hamming it up. He was certain a blush covered his face.

Her mouth dropped open as she saw hairs sprouting across his entire body. Hands and feet transformed into paws. A bushy tail appeared. A wolf sprang up in Conall's place, and bounded around his bedroom. In total surprise, her hand covered her mouth. "How did you do this?" she asked. "What a great FX effect!"

Conall had seldom felt so hurt and disappointed. She really did not get it.

Sadey placed her hand on his shoulder. "I do understand," she said. "It's just that when I get really nervous, I laugh and make jokes. I'm sorry. Now I know we each have a really big secret."

He said, "But mine is horrible."

Sadey hugged him, and Conall clung to her.

She whispered, "You aren't alone in having something to cover up. You know I'm a witch."

He added, "Yes, but nothing compares to my secret. Are you just trying to make me feel better?"

"Maybe," she said, "except, don't you remember me telling you about Mrs. Hunkley growing a mustache?"

Conall said, "So you understand, I guess."

She nodded. "I've felt guilty since I was old enough to know I was a witch."

"Whatever you are," he said, "is not as bad as becoming a werewolf. I dread the full moon every month."

"Does it just occur during a full moon?" she asked.

"Mostly, but it has also happened twice at other times of the month, when I got really mad. The scary thing is that I might hurt someone I care about."

"That bothers me, too," she said. "What if I accidentally put a mustache on one of my friends? It might not look bad on you, but what about Amber? I hate being a witch! And another thing," she said. "I have wanted a puppy for at least two years. But every time I almost get one, something keeps it from happening. Whatever I really want, I just never seem to get, and that's got to be because I'm a witch. And a bad one at that."

Conall felt guilty. He turned to close his computer.

"What is up with you?" she asked.

"I'm sorry," he said. "Dogs hate me. They chase me down the street and howl and bark when I'm nearby. If you got a puppy, I'd never get to come see you."

4: PUPPY SEARCH

SADEY SAID, "YOU COULD NEVER stop me from getting a puppy. It just turned out somebody always bought them first." Even as she said that, she felt a chill go down her back. "Well, if it was you, what'd you do with them? I know you didn't keep the puppies."

"They were unhurt." Conall could not bring himself to say more. He had taken them to the animal shelter. He was relieved to see that she seemed more surprised than angry. "You always got so excited that you told us every detail. What the puppy looked like, and where and when you were going to buy it."

"I *am* getting a dog," she said, "and you can't stop me. In fact, we're going to Salem *now*—together. You are driving, by the way. I might even make you buy this one for me." She smiled a devilish smile, and he thought maybe she *was* a witch after all.

"Okay," he agreed, "I'll buy the puppy, but we'll have to borrow my mom's car to get there and back."

THE VEHICLE CONALL "APPROPRIATED" FOR their drive to Salem was a hatchback. The rear seat was folded down, and the dog carrier Conall had acquired to transport each of the previous puppies was positioned in the back. Traveling east on Hwy 22, they were fully prepared for a successful purchase.

Sadey admitted, "I'm not as mad at you as I should be. Know why?"

"Nope," although he had noticed she wasn't furious with him. "So, why?"

"Partly, it's because you are helping me get a puppy. But mostly it's because I'm so relieved to find out being a witch has not been the cause of missing out on things I really want. And maybe, just maybe...I am learning to control my magic."

Her hair went into a ponytail, and then almost immediately came back out of it. Conall saw the motion from the corner of his eye. If only he had some positive outcome from becoming a werewolf. Her witchcraft was mild by comparison to his affliction. Mostly, her abnormality was related to fashion makeovers. She could change her clothes and hairstyle on a whim. She had even caused people to grow hair. That could potentially end baldness.

Conall thought about Sadey instantly becoming naked. If she really could do that, there might be a benefit for one of her male friends—namely, him.

"What are you grinning about now?" she asked.

"Oh, nothing. It just seems like becoming naked in the blink of an eye is a totally random thing."

"Not if that is what I daydream about. Do you really believe I wanted to be in the middle of a classroom wearing nothing but a skimpy bikini? All the guys stared at me. It was not random at all,"

She added. "Random is someone telling you for no reason that they drank their juice this morning. Is 'juice' some kind of code word for a special pomegranate drink or something? The new kid, Des, mentioned it to me just a few minutes ago. Now, *that* was random."

Conall turned partly away with a guilty look on his face, and said, "I thought, originally, the bikini incident was some kind of publicity stunt. You know, for becoming a swimsuit model or something." He was annoyed she had been talking to Des and wanted her to return to their previous topic.

"*Right,*" she said, not hiding her disgust. Then she added, "I never thought anyone would mistake me for a swimsuit model. Anyways, what am I supposed to believe about those antics on your bedroom floor? Was that meant to get *you* something special? Maybe a spot on the six o'clock news? It was you—and not me—who got naked instantly."

Ouch, he thought, and guessed it served him right. "I have no control at all over becoming a werewolf," he confessed. "It scares me. I become something inhuman—a beast. But I'm relieved I finally told you about it." In an attempt to divert their discussion away from him, he said, "What if you thought of a hot bath right now?" He was careful not to sound too eager. "Could all your clothes really disappear?"

"In your dreams," she said. "Actually, I think it makes more sense for me to experiment on making *other* people's clothes disappear. How would you like to be driving down the road naked right now?"

Conall kept his eyes on the highway as he again changed the subject. "Does it have to be a little dog? The puppy you get, I mean. The small ones seem to freak-out the most around me, and they yap all the time."

"Who is this dog for, anyway?" Sadey asked. When he remained silent, she added, "We'll try to pick one out that likes you too, okay?"

"Yes, that would be good if we can find one who does." he said.

Conall and Sadey were approaching downtown Salem, actually crossing over the Center Street Bridge, when Sadey saw a boy floundering in the Willamette River. It looked like the Jet Ski he'd been boating on had spilled and injured him. She pointed and yelled.

"Look."

Conall glanced across to see, then he nodded and sped up, making a right-hand turn onto the down ramp toward Front Street. At the second traffic signal, he veered into the parking area for Riverfront Park. Even so, seconds seemed like hours.

Conall glanced over at Sadey. He feared what she would think if she saw him as a wolf.

She studied him, as well. The look on her face indicated she saw something very different happening to his exterior.

Conall looked in the mirror. Hairs were popping out all over.

"You better get your clothes off," Sadey blurted.

It was most likely too late. Everything he was wearing had already been stretched to the point of breaking. Staring in the mirror, he saw his face elongating, and his teeth becoming fangs.

Looking calmer than she should, Sadey said, "Hurry...that kid won't last long."

She seemed to concentrate strongly on his pants and shirt, as if she might be picturing him without them. The confident look on her face indicated she knew she could do it.

He saw in the mirror that his clothing appeared in a neat pile resting atop the dog carrier in the back.

Sadey threw open her passenger-side car door and yelled, "Go and save him!"

The wolf sitting in Conall's place filled the entire front seat area. He leaped over her legs, and his fur brushed her face. Continuing on, he bounded across the paved area past two homeless men. They did not seem concerned by the presence of a wolf.

"Please be in time," Sadey called out as the hairy creature she knew as Conall disappeared past the carousel building, and raced toward the river—

MINUTES LATER, A DRENCHED WOLF loped back to the vehicle, scattering a flock of pigeons that had landed to forage in the grass. Sadey got out, and opened the door for the gigantic canine. He shook his shaggy coat, getting water all over her as she held the seat forward so he could jump into the back. With the dog carrier there, it was a tight fit. He made room for himself by shifting the carrier aside with his body. Then he turned in a circle and lay down.

Sadey got in the front passenger seat and closed the door as if putting a wolf in the car was an everyday occurrence. She noticed a boy staring in the rear window of the hatchback. When she adjusted the rearview mirror, she could see that Conall had mostly returned to normal. He struggled to pull his clothes on over his wet body.

Cracking her door open a few inches, Sadey called back to the curious kid, "He just loves to swim. Isn't it a beautiful day?"

The youngster walked off, shaking his head.

Fully clothed, Conall returned to the driver's seat. He continued their journey toward Lancaster Avenue by traveling up State Street four blocks, but then on an impulse he turned left, traveled another block, and in no time he turned left again onto Court Street.

Sadey had just said, "I guess I'm getting two dogs for the price of one today," and laughed. "You are paying for both of them, one way or another. And the one that is not a puppy, I don't even have to feed...or pick up after."

"Yuk, yuk," he said.

It came as a surprise to Sadey when he immediately pulled into a parking space in front of The Book Bin's storefront. "What are we doing here? They won't have dogs in a bookstore."

"But they'll have books on dogs, and that can help us to choose the right puppy." He was out of the car and walking toward the bookshop before she could reply.

Sadey thought he made quite a sight with his mussed-up, wet hair, and clothes that were so damp in places they clung to him oddly. Nevertheless, she followed him inside. They enquired of the young woman at the cash register about books on dogs, and angled left through the store. There were several volumes on how to choose and raise a puppy, including a couple of books for "idiots." After hastily glancing around, Conall left Sadey to make her pick, and went on his own quest. He asked the girl at the counter where he might find books on Werewolves, and she directed him over a couple of aisles to the right, in a section that also included fairies and vampires.

Sadey found a suitable puppy book, and Conall actually found what should be a helpful book on werewolves, with Lycanthropy in the title.

As they exited the bookstore, Sadey asked, "By the way, did you save the kid?"

"I guess so," Conall replied. "Once I change over from human, everything is hard to remember afterwards."

"The positive news is," she used a lighthearted voice, "you converted without wrecking your clothes—thanks to me. And you changed because you wanted to, not because you had to. This is daytime, and the full moon has already passed. Afterwards, you found your way back to the car." Sadey added, "Plus—and this is major—you did not *kill your best friend.*

"Oh, and..." she said in afterthought, "I used my magic on purpose, in a new way, and for the first time...it turned out really good." She smiled at him.

As they cruised through Salem, Conall absently turned on the radio, which was set to a local station his mom liked. He was about to switch to one of the more popular Portland stations when there was a news bulletin. The announcer interrupted to tell about a big dog swimming out into the Willamette River to save a drowning girl.

"I thought it was a boy," Sadey said.

"Who knows?" said Conall. "I thought there was something unexpected about the scent, but it was hard to tell in all that water. At least she is safe."

"The parents wish to give the '*dog*' a reward," Sadey said. "Do you want to change back so you can collect? If they just give you a dog biscuit, you can keep it. If they give you money...."

"We'll use it to pay for the puppy," he said. "No. We better stick to our original plan." He patted the pocket with his wallet in it and the credit card his mom allowed him to use. He would have some explaining to do about his purchase, just like some previous ones, but as long as he paid her back things should work out.

The pet store they stopped at first had only one puppy. When they passed by three kittens on the way to look at the puppy, the kitties hunched their backs like Halloween cats. They continued hissing until Conall was out of sight. And then a cluster of ferrets reacted even stronger to his presence—seeming to go crazy.

"See what I mean," he said, but Sadey focused on her search.

The only puppy available was a Labrador retriever crossbreed. Actually, it was a chocolate lab-mix, and had bluish eyes. It did not react to Conall the way he had feared. Instead, it curiously sniffed his hand."

"Sold!" Conall said.

Sadey smiled. "It's pretty big, though, I'm not sure what my folks will say."

"You can keep him on the back porch until he's housetrained."

"She," Sadey corrected. "We can keep *her* on the back porch... but what if she gets lonely, and howls?"

"Maybe we should buy a kitten to go with her?"

"No. My mom's allergic to cats."

On the way back home, with the puppy safely inside the carrier, Sadey said, "You know, it's almost as if the two of us together...."

She seemed uncertain how to finish her sentence.

"Complete each other?" he asked.

She said, "I like the word 'complement' better. This is the first time my magic turned out the way I wanted it to, when I saved your clothes from ripping apart, and then you did something really amazing with your ability, as well."

"I've always thought of it as a curse," he said, "not an ability."

"Somehow, when we're together," Sadey said, "both our previous burdens must combine in a way we can be proud of. Do you think something good like this could happen again? And would we have to be with each other? I mean, from now on, do we need to be together in order for things to work like they did today?"

"I guess so, unless you can remove my pants from a distance."

"We'll have to experiment and find out," she said. "I might begin by seeing if I can magically remove other boys' pants, first. What do you think? The possibilities are endless, but just for the sake of science, of course."

She smiled, obviously thinking about something she thought was funny.

Conall adjusted the rearview mirror and glanced at her face. "You look like you might be planning something—interesting."

"I simply wondered what it would be like if certain less-than-desirable dudes found themselves stranded naked in a Centrist High restroom. I'm thinking of a few really obnoxious types."

Conall said, "You wouldn't really do that."

"Just for an experiment," Sadey said. "To see if I can. This ability raises so many questions. For instance, do I need to be near someone for it to work? What happens to their clothes if I do not plan where they should end up?"

"Won't events like that draw attention to us?" Conall asked.

"Not if we don't tell anyone. Who's going to know, besides us?"

Conall shifted uneasily in his seat. It felt breezy all of a sudden. He didn't know why he seemed so uncomfortable. Glancing in the rearview mirror again, he saw Sadey had a broad smile on her face.

Her eyes moved meaningfully to the right, where she swung his boxer shorts round-and-round her index finger. Laughing uproariously, she said, "I'm getting the hang of this."

"Not funny," he said, knowing his face was red. "Put them back right now!"

He glanced down. They were on him again, only outside of his pants. "Knock it off, will you?" Conall then felt them on him again, but underneath his pants. They needed some adjusting, except he would not give her the satisfaction, and put up with the discomfort.

"How would you like it?" he asked, "if I could take your panties off like that?"

"You mean like this?" She thrust a pair of pink panties near his cheek. "Want to give them a spin?"

Conall started to jerk the steering wheel in surprise, but managed to keep the vehicle in its lane, and then he just shook his head. She better be careful or they'd get in an accident and it would be all her fault. He did not deserve that, and neither did the cute little puppy. Conall thought he heard her whisper, "You wuss."

5: DISAPPEARING DIAPER

*T*HE NEXT DAY, CONALL PICKED Sadey up on the way to school, and she rode on the back of his Yamaha 250cc motor scooter. It was almost impossible to talk through the rushing air—even with the benefit of a windshield. Plus, there was the thrum of the engine, and they were wearing helmets. Apparently to make up for that, when they parked, Sadey jabbered nonstop.

"So then," she paused to catch her breath, "I was babysitting Ethan. He is almost two, but he still wears diapers. Of course, you already knew that. Well, no one was around, so I decided to make his diaper disappear, and guess what?"

"You made *him* disappear instead," Conall said.

She gave Conall one of her, *Why don't you grow up?* looks, and said, "No. The diaper vanished, and went on the mantle just like I wanted it to, and you were not anywhere near. Do you think this means you can become a wolf whenever you want? Even without me close by?"

"Maybe, if I don't care about running around nude afterwards," he said. "I do not plan to try it."

She said, "The next time I babysit, when everyone else is gone, you come over and we'll do an experiment. You can go in the guest room, if you like. Transform, and see what happens to your clothes. Wear old ones, and bring a spare set, just in case."

"Are you sure you just don't want to see my bare buttocks again?" he asked.

The glaring look she gave him made the previous one seem mild. "This is for science," she said. But there was a little smirk on her lips, and her eyes twinkled.

"Right," he agreed, holding up his index finger, and rotating it as though he was twirling around a pair of underpants.

She laughed. "Nothing says science can't be fun."

"At my expense. How about I come over and watch you make all *your* clothes go on the mantle?"

"I'm not even going to answer a question like that," she said huffily. "We have to get to class now. See you fourth period."

They had separated by a few paces when Amber ran up to him. "Guess what?"

Conall started to say something mean. Her hair was a shade of orange that did not work for her complexion, or the clothes she wore. Lots of girls colored their hair, but none that he knew about did so as often as Amber. One day it might be purple with a blue swatch running through it. And the next, something totally different.

As nearly as he could remember, she'd started out as a sort of Goth girl. Black hair and clothes, dark eye shadow, and black nail polish. Then the color started creeping into her black hair. Every bright hue a person could ever imagine, including chartreuse and crimson.

As he thought more about it, he could not recall what her natural hair color was. Her current shade of orange was the worst of all. But, to be honest, Amber just had that effect on him lately, something about her always rubbed him the wrong way.

Nevertheless, he somehow managed not to say anything really unkind, for the moment. "What?" he asked Amber.

"Des likes me!" she shouted. "We're going out—I think."

Sadey was near enough to hear, and stopped short. "What?"

"He said he wants to take me to some hidden place here at school, and do things to me no one's ever done before."

Sadey said, "He asked you out?"

"Well, I guess so. Isn't that what we would be doing, going out?"

Sadey did not appear to have an answer. The look on her face was hard for Conall to read, but she seemed to have conflicting feelings. "Maybe you *are* going out," she said. "But you might want to clarify that with Des, just to be certain."

"Good idea," Amber replied with relief. She left in a hurry, and it seemed to Conall like she might have thought her revelation about Des would cause Sadey to yell at her.

"There is something about that guy I don't like," Conall said.

Sadey replied, "He's okay. He just tries too hard. He doesn't have many friends, being a new kid in school. That's tough."

"I can't say I ever really hated anybody," said Conall. "But I have a bad feeling in my bones about this guy, and it wouldn't take much for me to hate him."

Sadey felt something deep inside, as well. It was not hatred, but just as strong. Perhaps it was a mixture of fear and excitement? A chill went through her, and she reached out and took Conall's hand. "Walk me to class, will you?"

"I have to go to my locker first, and I don't want to be late. There isn't time."

"Please!"

He knew Sadey didn't like to beg.

She moved closer to him and whispered in his ear, "I might be so grateful, all my clothes would go to the mantle."

He knew that was a lie, but it showed how much she wanted him with her in that moment. "Okay," he said. "Can I bring my camera to record the clothes-less event?"

She hit him. "Ow!" she said, "That really hurt—*me.*"

"I'd say it serves you right," he said, "but then you might harm yourself again, even worse."

She raised her fist, but thought better of it.

Conall carried her books as they headed into the school. How friendly were she and Des? The way that guy looked at Sadey and Amber caused Conall major concern.

AS THE BIG WOLF SLUNK silently from the hallway into the living room, Sadey held her breath. She had locked her puppy, Hershey, safely in her bedroom. There was a moment of uncertainty as her brother Ethan noticed the wolf.

Standing still, the twenty-two-month-old stared. The huge canine-like beast moved slowly forward, towering above the toddler. Ethan's little arm rose, and pointed. If he screamed in fright, how would the werewolf react? Sadey whispered, "Maybe this experiment wasn't such a good idea." She tried to move between them, but the wolf leapt, keeping her separated from Ethan. The toddler's small arm still extended, but a shocked look covered his face.

"Conall," said Sadey in her softest voice. "Please don't—"

The massive wolf rolled onto his side. His feet pointed in the air, and the large head lolled toward Ethan. The animal's giant pink tongue flopped out, and his sharp fangs glinted, but the tongue softened their affect.

41

Ethan laughed, closing the distance between them, and threw himself on the big canine's chest, shouting, "Doggie!"

Apparently, he was so used to playing with Hershey it was an easy transition to the wolf, despite its larger size. The two wrestled on the floor, and the werewolf's play-snarling always ended with a puppyish yelp.

Hershey could be heard scratching the inside of Sadey's bedroom door. What if the chocolate Lab got out? If Hershey remained in her room, how would Sadey's mother react to the scratches on the door?

With a final look at the tussling twosome, Sadey went to liberate Hershey.

Conall had said he thought the big puppy and the werewolf would get along because it had liked him from the first. Other dogs definitely did not.

Hershey joined the scuffling on the floor, making it a three-way tangle. They were having so much fun, Sadey looked jealous. Still, she did not join them. She sat on the couch and laughed at their antics. Ethan had his arms around the huge, hairy neck, while Hershey growled and tugged on the wolf's shaggy tail.

None of the three seemed to wear out. Finally, Sadey said, "Conall, it is time to change back. Please go in the guest-room."

The wolf's head turned toward her as if to complain, obviously not wanting to stop. Hershey paid no attention to Sadey's commands to "sit." Instead, she raced helter-skelter about the room. The big puppy even bounced across the couch cushions once. But when Hershey returned to where the wolf had been—*there lay Conall.*

As if an animal changing into a person happened daily, Hershey took up playing with Conall, fully clothed, where she'd left off with the wolf, except there was no tail to pull.

Isolating Hershey in the bedroom with a new bone was the strategy Sadey utilized. And giving Ethan a snack, she let him sit on the couch to eat it, which also worked. That was a definite no-no by parental rules, but eventually Sadey created a peaceful time for talking with Conall.

"Why," he asked her, "Can't *you* disappear and reappear. You do it with clothes and other things. The principle should be the same for people, and what they wear."

"Why didn't I think of that? I would have to be careful to take a change of clothes for such an experiment. Otherwise, you might get a real eyeful. In theory, I could take my clothes along with me."

Sitting on the floor together, Sadey and Conall undertook the new challenge. She focused on a spot in front of the fireplace, but then seemed to have a different idea. When she disappeared, Conall stared at the spot where she'd been sitting.

He was beginning to worry when she reappeared near the fireplace still fully clothed.

Conall saw her startled look, as she found herself standing over by the mantle a few feet away.

"Wow," he said. "You really did it."

Apparently Ethan was too interested in his snack to notice.

Sadey transported Conall beside her, also fully clothed. Before he had time to adjust, she projected them both onto the couch, to the left of Ethan. Her little brother pointed at them, and then to the fireplace, and returned to eating his treat.

"Yes," Sadey said, looking back over at the empty brickwork.

Conall realized Ethan was too young to understand what he had seen. Even if he did realize its occurrence, he could not describe it to anyone. Others would think he was talking gibberish. To be safe, though, he thought Sadey should be more careful in future experiments, and not do such things in front of Ethan. "I call that 'taking it to the next level,'" Conall said.

She smiled broadly at him. "Next level..." she said thoughtfully, as though it had two meanings.

"Where did you vanish to, at first?"

"I went to my bedroom, so that if my clothes didn't come with me, I'd still have something to put on, and you wouldn't be sitting there gawking at me."

"That was a good idea," he said.

Sadey added, "I love having you here, but it'll be awkward if my folks come home and find us together like this."

Conall ruffled Ethan's hair, and rose to leave without protesting.

Pausing just before he closed the entrance door to her house, he said, "I am a little worried about what might happen next."

6: SPECIAL MISSION

CONALL TOLD SADEY, "I DON'T want to," at school on Monday. "I must get to my locker." He moved hurriedly on past her.

"We need this checked out," she said, "and the restroom is right there. It won't take you a minute."

He knew it would waste more time debating than if he just did what she wanted. "Okay," he said, "but you owe me."

"Hurry," she demanded.

When he went through the door into the boy's lavatory, he immediately noticed how quiet it was. There was no one present, and he turned to leave.

"Hey," came a whisper behind him.

Conall turned around. There was a boy's face partially visible, peeking out from one of the stalls.

"Come here."

Conall moved slowly closer, and the face became one he recognized. It belonged to the school's biggest bully, nicknamed Blizzard. He'd gotten his name from rubbing kid's noses in sweet treats they got at ice cream drive-ins.

"We need you to go get us some clothes."

Conall glanced around at the empty room.

"Guys," Blizzard hissed. "Show yourselves—*now.*"

Faces popped out of the other stall doors.

Conall deduced there were three naked bullies hiding in the boy's restroom. He smiled even though he tried not to.

"It ain't funny!" Blizzard said.

"Well," Conall said, "I don't know where I can find your clothes."

Blizzard began to emerge from the stall where he had been hiding. "We'll just start by taking yours, then."

Conall saw the large unclothed body moving toward him, and then it was gone, completely missing. No sign remaining. All the other faces had vanished as well.

Back in the hallway, Conall found Sadey with her hand over her mouth, trying to hide her laughter. There were screams down the hall as girls ran out from their restroom as if a fire roared inside.

Conall saw a woman teacher make her way inward after a short huddle with a distraught female student. A moment later, she came running out, and pulled a cell phone from her pocket.

Conall could guess she was calling the main office to get an administrator, although she might be calling 911, as well.

Sadey grabbed his hand. "Come on. You need to get to your locker, remember?"

"You set me up," he complained.

"I just wanted to be sure it would work. It was a scientific experiment—to benefit mankind—but mostly womankind".

"Well, it's *my* face they saw," said Conall, "not yours. They are going to look for someone to get even with, and most likely, it will be me."

"That would not be wise," she said. "I wouldn't want to pick a fight with a guy who can turn into a werewolf whenever he wants to, especially not one whose best friend is a witch. The things we could do to them." She gave him a wicked grin.

Conall thought she was enjoying her experiments just a little bit too much. "We'll see," he said.

7: NEXT LEVEL?

*T*RUE TO HIS FAMILY CODE NAME—Des the Destroyer—he'd carefully planned his moment. Amber was such a fool to meet him alone in the secluded woodlot. The cemetery was barely visible through the trees, and its graveyard would literally be Amber's last resting place. Perhaps he would prop her lifeless form against a tombstone. He smiled at the image in his mind, and enjoyed picturing her blank eyes and pale white skin with faint traces of liquid red on her neck.

She was currently full of life, however, and when Des took her in his arms, she seemed aware only of her infatuation with him. She responded so completely, he felt mild guilt. Not enough to keep him from kissing her passionately in return, however, because she would be *his first.*

Amber's excitement nearly matched his own. Perhaps he should only turn her to the dark side. His family could use her as a servant, and perpetual blood donor. No. He wanted her the old-fashioned way. It was an established family tradition.

Des tilted Amber's head to the side. He pulled her hair back, and she moaned with pleasure as he kissed her on the neck. He felt her pulse pounding against his lips. She was so ripe, so ready. His mother's idea of making love the normal way, and culminating with the blood sucking—was a big temptation.

Nevertheless, he could not wait that long. It would be agonizing, trying to drag out her death. Des would kill her now—with one long, delicious bite. Her ecstasy would be complete, though short-lived. More importantly, *his* ecstasy would be more phenomenal than anything he'd experienced previously.

"Starting without me?" whispered a familiar voice.

Des looked up, keeping his lips at his victim's neck. This could not be happening.

Oblivious to the newcomer, Amber moaned with delight.

A male form moved nearer. Des could not believe the interruption of his *first time*, and by his own father! Des glared at the man who resembled an angelic teenage male.

"You must take your time," said his parent. "We can each nibble opposite sides of her neck."

How disgusting was that—sharing his first kill? His dad couldn't take equal part in this sacred initiation. Des was incensed. His lips pulled an inch away from her jugular and he snarled, "Stay back. She's mine."

"There is plenty for both," the parental tone was reasonable. "Without me, you will rush, and ruin the experience."

"Who is this?" Amber asked, pulling slightly away from Des.

"No one," Des hissed. He dared not proceed, because he could not take his eyes off his father.

"Is he another new student?" Amber sounded intrigued. "Does he want me, too?"

"Very much," whispered the handsome young man moving still closer.

Des had bent her over backward, but he let her collapse to the ground. There was only one way to deal with his father. The growing blood lust propelled Des forward. Visibly, they were nothing more than two blurs across the forest floor.

Amber whispered, "They both want me."

Only when they locked in combat did their motion slow enough so she could see what was actually occurring. It was every girl's dream-come-true, two hot guys fighting it out to see which would win her. There could not be a greater aphrodisiac. Amber sighed.

A third streaking form appeared out of nowhere. When it stopped, there was a lovely teenage female. She had a very unpleasant look on her face. "Boris. What are you doing? It is little Desi's first time. Let him have his fun."

The two males paused in their conflict.

"He's ruining it," Des complained.

His father said, "He's botching this whole thing."

"Then let him," said the girl. "You did the same with yours, if I recall correctly. He has to learn in his own way. Come home, now."

She stepped forward, glaring at her mate. "Now!

To complicate matters even further, two other teenagers materialized beside Amber. Sadey appeared first, and took her friend's arm before pulling her to her feet. "Come on."

Amber resisted.

Conall said with strong exasperation in his voice, "They are going to kill you if you don't come with us."

The three vampires stared at the newcomers. Des's father stepped forward, but his mother, Natasha, halted her youthful-appearing consort. "No, Boris. You are coming with me. Our son can handle this by himself. What a glorious thing. Imagine...a triple sacrifice for his first trophy hunt." She grabbed Boris' arm and whisked him away.

"You are ruining it." Amber shook free of Sadey. "Leave us. You're just jealous." Amber's anger at Sadey turned into confusion as Des streaked toward them unbelievably fast—and Conall shape-shifted into an enormous wolf.

Conall had changed instantly into his wolf form, but he moved slowly as he circled Des. Not in complete circles—but repeating semi-circles that kept him between the two girls and the vampire. Des was perhaps faster. Nevertheless, the wolf's cunning anticipated each of the vampire's next moves. Their swift actions became no more than smudges in the air. Additionally, they utilized trees and uneven terrain, making it difficult for Sadey to track them.

Amber yelled, "Stop! What's going on?"

In that moment, and for the first time when he'd shapeshifted, Conall knew he was more than a wolf. He was a human in canine form, with full awareness of both aspects of himself.

He barely noticed Sadey make Amber disappear. Undoubtedly, she had been instantly flung across the miles to her distant room—hopefully now a haven of rest and safety. But Conall had more to worry about than that, or even his battle with Des.

Remaining focused on avoiding Des, Conall kept him away from Sadey. He felt no pain, but occasional contact of sharp teeth with his hairy body left red swatches on nearby brush and grass. It took only a few moments for Conall to know there were two more bodies in motion about him. The vampire's parents had returned, making significant gashes in his coat and staining his fur red.

There were some Conall-inflicted, red stained rips in Des' clothing as well. However, if something didn't change to even the odds against him, Conall would not survive for long. He moved into thicker brush to make it harder for the other three to harm him. His strength was draining, but then he noticed something that caused a glimmer of hope.

Sadey had apparently anticipated where one of the vampires would be next as it zoomed toward Conall. She appeared just to its side, and pushed the vampire off-course into a nearby tree. That one turned out to be Des. He fell to the ground unconscious after a sickening thud against the trunk of a stout oak.

Conall glimpsed the she vampire hurtling toward him. So intent was Natasha on killing him, she did not see danger until it was too late. Sadey materialized beside her, and a well-timed push sent the vampire headlong into another substantial oak where she crumpled unconscious to the ground. She lay there with her lethal vampire teeth glinting clearly from her open mouth.

The odds had reversed. Sadey and Conall outnumbered the remaining vampire. He apparently didn't realize that, yet, and Conall knew Sadey must act before the last male vampire grasped his situation, since total surprise was her greatest weapon.

The vampire raced a zigzag course around the much-slowed wolf. Conall could not last long. In fact, his head drooped badly. He could not help it; blood loss had reached the critical stage.

Des' father began his killing run. Conall sensed it, but had no strength to turn in time to put up a fight. His battle was over, and he had lost.

Sadey appeared at Boris' side and angled him into a mighty fir tree. The woods resounded with the crash. Conall glimpsed the outcome from the side of his eye, even as he slumped down, breathing with difficulty. His final conscious image was of the bodies of all three vampires crumpled on the ground, unmoving.

Conall felt Sadey appear at his side, and her hand stroked the fur of his muzzle even as his eyes glazed. His body shuddered. His once powerful legs had totally given out.

He heard her scream, "No!" and felt her arms encircle his upper body as he lost consciousness.

When he next became aware, Sadey held him, bloodied and nearly lifeless, in the waiting room of a local veterinarian's office where they had taken Hershey for his puppy shots.

"Please help," she hollered.

Seldom had there been such a commotion in that room.

Patrons fled the facility with their whining and meowing pets, while the trained helpers rallied to save the badly injured wolf, and

Conall lost consciousness again.

It was only later that he learned how Sadey had returned to the woodland battle scene, but with a quick stop on the way. She'd made a side-trip to a building construction lot. There, she'd obtained three wooden stakes used for laying out the new house foundation.

In the old deserted cemetery near the woodlot, Sadey selected a massive grave marker that declared in large letters REST IN PEACE. She quickly materialized each of the three vampires before the headstone, and positioned them side-by-side on the ground with a wooden stake on their chest, resting carefully over their hearts.

Sadey later told Conall that she assumed they would get the message. If not, her back-up plan was a more permanent solution. For reasons she did not understand, Sadey could not bring herself to kill Des. She hoped that was not a mistake. If it were necessary, she could easily dispose of the other two vampires without self-recrimination. They would only get the one chance, so they must take it, or die.

THE FOLLOWING MORNING, CONALL LAY in human form at home on his bed, recuperating from his injuries. His Smartphone rang on his nightstand, and he groaned loudly as he leaned over to answer it.

"Did I wake you, Conall?" said Sadey.

"Oh," he groaned. "Yes. Where are you?"

"I was walking through the school halls in a daze, wondering how you're doing. You going to be all right?"

"Yeah," he replied, "Thanks to you."

"I don't think I can survive the entire day without seeing you," her voice spilled from his phone. "Can I come over later?" Without awaiting his reply she said, "Amber's not speaking to me. I haven't seen Des since I left him in the cemetery. He seemed somehow at home in the shadow of the grave marker. I wish I'd taken a picture with my cell phone. Probably wouldn't have been a good idea, though."

There was a pause before she whispered, "There's Des now, walking right toward me. He doesn't see me with all the kids in the way....

"Whew...he went on by without spotting me. I kind of liked him, but I like keeping my blood even more. Well, I better get to class—see you later."

Conall let his phone drop on the bed and groaned. "Later." The pain was really getting to him. He was so sore he could barely move. He hoped Sadey did not call him back any time soon.

He lay with his eyes closed. His mother had somehow bought Sadey's story of a bicycle accident having caused him to roll down a blackberry-covered hillside. He briefly wondered what had become of Amber. Did she have any idea how close she'd come to ending up as a bloodless corpse?

He was lucky to be alive. Would the vampires leave him alone? Had they all survived their crashes into trees? Well, Des had, so probably the other two were alive, as well.

Conall drifted off to sleep again, knowing that in his condition, if a vampire showed up, he could not fight back.

It seemed like only a minute later when his phone rang.

"Did I wake you?" Sadie asked.

"Yes," he replied.

"Sorry. It's lunchtime, and I do not have anyone to eat with. I can't sit with Amber. I sure can't sit near Des. I'm afraid if I go anywhere else, someone will ask me what is going on with us. Why you're not at school, and all that. I can't say...." Her voice became a conspiratorial whisper, "Well, over the weekend I helped a werewolf fight off three vampires, and saved a girl from getting all her blood sucked out. They'd think I'm crazy."

Conall didn't need to answer. She just kept talking.

"Since you are awake, now, I'm going to pop in and see how you are doing. Okay?"

She apparently took his silence for a yes, because Conall was smiling weakly as he looked up into her eyes. "Aren't you supposed to be in school?" he whispered.

"I'm taking a part-day off, visiting a sick friend."

He whispered, "This isn't over, you know."

"You may be right. Perhaps we better make it turn out the way we want."

"How?" he groaned.

She glanced through the window with a distant look in her eye. "Maybe we should all get together and have a little talk."

"I'm not getting out of bed for at least a day." He thought it might be more like a week, or even a month.

Sadey said, in a voice he found disgustingly cheerful, "Then, we'll have a conference right here. Oh, I almost forgot. What did your folks say?"

He searched his mind until the memories came back. "Oh, they are making the best of their unplanned Hawaiian vacation."

"Right. It slipped my mind," she said sweetly. "How are they enjoying their all-expense paid holiday?"

"They haven't called since you talked to them with my cell phone and convinced them I'm all right, and recovering rapidly from a few scratches."

Sadey chuckled. "They never won anything big like that before, did they? They deserve a rest, and so do you. Get ready. I'm bringing some guests over."

Des appeared in the middle of Conall's room, looking disoriented. Amber soon followed. She was so bewildered, she collapsed on the floor.

Conall watched the two suspiciously. He was too weak to defend himself if anything went wrong.

Sitting beside Conall, Sadey said to Des, "Time to talk."

Des glared at her. His muscles tightened, and he lowered into a half-crouch. When he snarled, his fangs seemed to lengthen. It looked like he would spring toward her.

"Chill out," she said.

Conall watched through swollen eyelids as Des disappeared.

"We will give him a moment to cool off," Sadey said conversationally. "How's your morning going so far, Amber?"

Their former friend did not respond.

"Oh, sorry to interrupt," said Sadey, although no one else was talking. "I better bring him back, or he might...."

Conall watched as Des emerged from nothingness, with his arms clutching his chest. He had frost at the edges of his mouth.

"I understand," Sadey commented, "that vampires don't feel the cold like the rest of us. The South Pole was just a hint of what I can do to you and your parents if you don't cooperate."

Des seemed impressed. Through chattering teeth he asked, "What do you want?"

Shifting her position on the bed, and taking hold of Conall's hand, Sadey replied to Des, "We can't be friends, obviously. I want to make a deal with your family. You leave us alone, and that includes ungrateful Amber over there. In turn, we will leave you alone. Sound fair?"

Des remained silent.

"How long can you hold your breath? Sadey asked him.

Conall saw concern on Des' face.

"Do you deal well with lots of pressure?" Sadey asked. "You

52

know, the kind you will experience a mile under the ocean surface. Maybe pressure is not your thing?"

Conall could see her line of reasoning was making an impact on the vampire.

"Or...the moon might be nice this time of year," Sadey said pleasantly. "No tourists. Only a little gravity, but no oxygen to speak of. The best part, from my perspective, there is no blood—except your own, before it freezes. I think I remember from science class that the dark side of the moon stays a couple of hundred degrees below zero. That was probably Fahrenheit, not that it would matter to you that much, once you are there."

"Boris and Natasha have moved," said Des. "They left me here alone."

It sounded odd to Conall, the way the vampire referred to his parents by their first names.

Sadey asked, "Can you contact them?"

Des nodded.

"Let them know about this deal we are willing to make. It is a one-time offer. The wooden stakes were a warning. I may be squeamish about pounding them through your black hearts. Nevertheless, I have no trouble sending you away. The places I select will have no return flights."

"Okay," said Des. "I don't really have anywhere else to go. They paid off the house and left me plenty of money. I'm not a very good vampire, anyway. I disgraced my family when I botched my first kill." He looked at Amber. "She was supposedly a sure thing."

"Fine," said Sadey. "We'll make appearances seem normal between us, and I'll talk to you in the school halls. You can even sit with me at lunch, occasionally. Just don't forget our treaty, ever— not even for a second."

"I agree."

Conall wondered if this wasn't all going too smoothly. Could they believe Des?

Sadey smiled at Des just before he disappeared from the room.

Conall asked, "What about Amber?"

Their ex-friend looked up from the floor where she sat in a dejected heap. "Please don't send me to the moon," she begged.

At least *she'd* gotten the message, Conall thought.

"You are no threat to us," said Sadey. "Keep it that way. Not a word about any of this to anyone or I will send you far away. How does Afghanistan sound? An insurgent stronghold, perhaps?

Somewhere they really hate Americans."

Amber shivered. "Please don't."

"It is your choice. Maybe, if you keep your mouth shut, we can be friends again some day.

Amber disappeared, and Conall let his swollen eyes close.

"I'm tired," Sadey said. "Move over, will you? All of this transporting people around has worn me out. Got any juice?"

He mumbled, "I got a little bit of the red stuff left in me, but I plan to keep that."

"I'm keeping mine, too," said Sadey. She closed her eyes and snuggled closer to her only friend—an injured werewolf.

She went to sleep almost immediately.

There was no way for either of them to know it at that time, but in the not too distant future, they would become uneasy allies with Des. The three of them would join forces, and undertake something so important, so difficult and dangerous, no one could guess the outcome.

However, that is another story you'll encounter in Book III of this volume.

The End

(Of book one. Turn the page for book two.)

BOOK TWO

VAMPIRE INDEPENDENCE

1: THE HUNT
—BEGINS *BEFORE* the Sadie Hawkins Dance—

*D*ES WAS THE LOOKOUT, AND his dad was the hunter who could pass for Des' slightly older brother. His mom was not with them for once. She always made things easier. Their current victim was a fifteen-year-old girl, quite pretty, actually, if one was into that sort of thing. Des was not.

Malls were perfect. His father, Boris, had lured this lovely female teen into a narrow access hallway. There were no surveillance cameras in there. The vampires had previously sealed the door at the opposite end so that employees would not disturb their trap.

Upstairs in the food court, the girl had warmed up to Des first, probably because he was less pushy and seemed non-threatening. Boris had gotten around that, as usual. He had said, "Unless you would rather make-out with this *kid* here. My *younger* brother."

What girl would choose that? Certainly not their intended one.

The bait Boris invariably used began with his *youthfulness.* That plus the supposed fact he was the youngest modeling agent in Salem always did the trick. He showed her the glossy publicity photos. He also had a fake I.D., and the business cards to go with it, plus an entire portfolio of his work, which was quite impressive.

Coincidentally, there was a real vampire movie shooting in Portland, and the producers were reportedly looking for more extras. According to Boris, it just happened there was a bit part requiring a girl—but she had to be a beauty. They needed a vampire to kill her, and the audience to be sympathetic.

All the girls Des and his dad had used this scam on had gotten literally eaten up by it. The foolish chicks all wanted to be models or movie stars, and needed to hear how beautiful they appeared. They were so pathetic and vulnerable that their hunger for reassurance, and possible "discovery" caused them to take unnecessary chances. Fortunately for Des, his parents were experts. No bodies ever surfaced—well, almost never. The local newscasts would sometimes report another missing child.

Boris had a phony video camera. It was behind the temporary, black plastic barrier, like the backdrops that legitimate photographers used. This particularly pretty girl was dealing with a pro, but not the type of professional she thought. Boris had seduced innocent girls for decades, but not in the normal sense. Romance was just one more of his predatory ploys.

Des followed all the details with his super hearing. She started to have second thoughts. Especially, when the kissing ended and it was time for the vampire fangs to descend on her neck.

His father told her, "They are just movie props, these fangs. Like at Halloween, only better."

Des heard her say "Oh…yeah."

Boris asked if she was certain she had never been in a movie before. Hadn't he seen her in…?

That is when he bit her. There was a sudden intake of breath. And a shocked yell that never got out because his hand covered her mouth. Then she succumbed. It almost sounded as if she enjoyed it. No girl ever survived for Des to ask. He heard her legs do their death-tap from convulsions. He knew from experience that Boris carefully saved every drop of liquid after his initial gulps. The family had to eat.

Des was likewise skilled at his job. He spotted the private security cop fifty-feet away. The guy was headed toward them, and had begun using his radio. Des moved rapidly to cut the man off.

Which ploy to utilize? The guard looked like the type who took his job way too seriously.

"Excuse me," Des said in a weak voice. "Three gang members cornered me and…." He dropped to the floor, holding his side. There were tears in his eyes. "I'm sorry. I'm not usually a baby." Des nodded up the stairs toward the next level. "I think they went up there. If you hurry, you can catch them."

The guy looked at him with concern. He would not leave someone he thought was seriously injured, but would instead call for backup. Des wasn't worried, he'd handled worse situations.

"I'll be fine," Des reassured. "They just knocked the wind out of me."

A while ago, Des knew, there had been gang shootings in the Lancaster Mall. Having gangbangers on the loose in a downtown mall was not a good thing. The store cop called in Des' report after Des added a description of three kids he had actually seen go to the second floor. That should keep security busy, and Des said, "Go ahead, I'll come along when I catch my breath."

Once the guard believed Des was not badly injured, he raced for the stairs.

Probably new, Des thought, and smiled, thinking one should *never* lose track of a prime witness.

By the time he got back to help Boris, the equipment and the body were secure in two big roller cases. The father and son team put on casual expressions. Then pushed their burdens toward the nearest entrance. Des would guard their things at the curb while his father brought the van around for loading everything. The hunt had not taken long. Boris didn't even ask about the security incident. Des was fine with that; it had all, especially his part, become simply routine.

*D*ES WAS AN ONLY CHILD whose close-knit family maintained peculiar old-world traditions and beliefs, customs that most typical American communities did not appreciate. That was the reason his family kept a *really big* secret. To complicate things even more, Des had an awful secret just his own, which he hid from his parents. For that reason, he thought of himself as a deviant. Someone very abnormal—even in his peculiar family.

Des had a remarkably pale complexion. He was blond, with intense green eyes. In height, he was tall as Sadey—the girl he had a crush on at his new school. He was short for a guy, but that didn't bother him because Des made up for it by being generally outgoing. Born Desiderio Bela Lugosi, he naturally preferred people call him by the nickname, Des.

He was descended from the *Old-line,* the ancient and very rare strain of vampires not light sensitive. A trait that came in especially handy.

Sitting at home by the breakfast table, Des did not worry about how he'd had to change schools in his sophomore year. That was not the big deal for him it would be for most students. Centrist High School in Independence, Oregon was not undersized, although it was significantly smaller than the one he had attended in Portland.

Des had the knack of fitting-in wherever his family moved. Before the last year in Portland, he had attended public school in Salem. Prior to that, he'd lived in Eugene. His parents moved around a lot, and for a very good reason.

"Don't be late for school," his mother said to Des in a sweet voice. She was much younger-looking than the parents of his classmates. She and his father could actually pass for his teenage siblings. Often, they pretended to be his peers, especially during trips to bigger cities.

"Yes, Natasha," he replied, thinking he was never late. His parents insisted he use their first names at all times. In that way, he would not mess up when the family hunted in Salem or elsewhere. He continued reading his chemistry book without looking at her.

She set a fabric lunch box beside him on the table, "I put your favorites in here again today, dear. Did you drink all your juice this morning?"

"Yes." He gestured at the empty glass—his proof—resting just beyond his chemistry book.

Juice was their family code word for blood. They used the term exclusively so they would never screw up in public. Again, he did not glance at her. Closing his book, and grabbing his lunch, Des tried to leave for school.

"Not so fast young man," said his mother.

Des dutifully went over and gave her a little kiss on her bared neck.

"You are growing up so fast, dear," she said with a wistful look at him. "Before we know it, you will be hunting your own food." She looked searchingly at him. "If you aren't already."

She chuckled. "You will give those pretty girls a thrill they never expected. Now, hurry and don't be late." She pushed him toward the door. "I have a very busy day ahead of me. You may have to get your own supper. There are plenty of vials in the fridge."

His mother was a phlebotomist who *loved* her work. Des had looked that word up when he was younger. The dictionary said a phlebotomist was a person who made incisions or punctures in human veins to draw blood. Des had no specific idea what his father did—something or other at the mortuary where his father worked part-time in Salem, and where he also "hunted."

"I love you," his mother said as Des opened the front entrance.

He repeated back his standard response, "Love you too, Mom," and quickly closed the door behind him.

He lived far enough from school to ride the bus, and he caught it regularly, just two blocks from home. Except for today, when he planned to walk. He had some thinking he needed to do. The crowded bus was not a good place for that.

Recently, doubts had filled Des' mind. He was attracted to girls as potential food sources, but nothing like his pull toward Sadey. Amazingly, his attraction to her was unrelated to blood lust. It was something different—unexplainable. He had not experienced that type of longing before.

Unfortunately, she already had a boyfriend, and something about Conall rang a warning bell in Des' mind. He knew that Conall was more dangerous than an enemy vampire in a rival clan would be. He just didn't know why or how he possessed that knowledge.

Part of the effect Sadey had on Des was that he now despised his family secret. He wanted to be more than a hunter of humans. Lately, he had taken to dumping his "juice" down the toilet when his mother was not watching. He had used the potted plant at first, but his mother became suspicious and started sniffing around. She had an acute sense of smell, even for a vampire.

His father, Boris, was seldom home. When not at the mortuary, he was prowling for food. His preferred victims were teenage girls. Boris had a seductive way about him the young females simply could not resist. He was impatient for Des to assume an adult role, because he wanted his son to be the greatest lady-killer in the history of their family—and it was a long and illustrious history.

Des looked up at the sign announcing he had arrived at Centrist High. Walking through the parking lot, a female voice hailed him. Looking over, he saw Sadey's friend, Amber.

She came running. "Looks like you are feeling better now," she said. "Did you get the picture I sent you?"

Des nodded, although he had not bothered to open her e-mail. He had told her he did not feel well yesterday, to get rid of her.

She leaned conspiratorially closer, "I hear you went to Sadey's."

Her natural aroma was overpowering. Des wanted nothing less than to take her around the corner and show her things the like of which she had never dreamt. In fact, he wanted to end her dreaming forever.

"Yes," he replied, "I went to Sadey's, but she wasn't home." He had left a note, but now, thoughts about Sadey made him want nothing to do with Amber, luscious as she smelled.

"Got to go," he said, and hurried away.

"Will you be at the dance?" she called after him.

He replied without turning around, "Possibly."

She whispered, "See you there."

He heard her, of course. His ears were exceptional sense organs. He simply did not respond. Maybe he would find Sadey in the halls. Moments later, Des saw Sadey twenty feet ahead. She was moving in his same direction, and he closed the gap. He proceeded with caution, to be certain her boyfriend, Conall, was not present. An envelope dropped out of Sadey's book bag, causing Des to flit forward, and snatch it up from the floor.

Inspecting the squarish surface, he decided it held some kind of greeting card, or invitation. It was unsealed, and he continued walking as he opened and read it. Des kept one eye on Sadey, just in case. Her card was an invitation, which read:

Conall,
Please come to the Sadie Hawkins dance with me.
Your friend, Sadey

Des placed it back in the envelope, and hurried so he could return it to her. "Excuse me, but I think you dropped this."

She absently looked it over, thanked him, and walked on. A few steps later, she turned and thanked him again. It was as if she did not remember doing so before. She didn't call him by name, nor did she seem to recognize Des.

"See you at the dance," he called as she entered a classroom.

Her hand rose in acknowledgment, but she did not turn and look at him.

Des raced to his own class with excitement filling him. He had actually talked to her without her boyfriend glaring at him from nearby. Des would see her at the Sadie Hawkins event, but what would he wear?

Although Des did not go out for sports, he was amazingly athletic. He was also an accomplished dancer. He could watch and copy the most elaborate routines, instantly.

Sitting in class, he daydreamed of eating lunch with Sadey. If only Conall would not be there. Maybe Des should go to the restroom and prank call Sadey. He had downloaded a fake voice-calling program. No, he couldn't risk it. She might find out, and block him from ever calling her again.

He had coaxed her number out of Amber, and Sadey didn't know he had it. He'd obtained her address in the same way. He had even gone to her house on the outskirts of Independence. In fact, Des went there almost every evening, and hung around after dark, hoping to catch a glimpse of her through a window.

He had actually entered her house, even her bedroom, where he'd watched her sleep. He longed to lie beside her, and he needed to face it, he was obsessed with the girl. Des went into the guy's restroom, and took out his phone.

Thanks again to Amber, he had also secured Sadey's password to her e-mail account. He looked down through her messages, checked a few new ones, and then marked each as unread.

Amber was the girl who was closest to Sadey. They chatted regularly, and he checked Sadey's Facebook account through Amber's contact. Amber was so obliging that she simply told Des anything he wanted to know about Sadey. She also told him things he did not want to know. Like, how friendly Sadey was with Conall.

Des checked the tracking device planted in Sadey's phone. Again, that was thanks to Amber. He had made her believe it was an "accelerator" to improve cell phone reception. Amber helped Sadey stick it on her phone's battery, with the result that Des knew Sadey's location wherever she went.

Maybe he should be a detective. But, basically, it was what smart vampires did, shadowing someone, and becoming part of their life. Learning their routines, until...that final moment of climax. Taking time for their first kill was a tradition in his family. "Quickies" were for the lowborn, or the newly-turned vampires.

Sadey was currently in the girl's restroom. He moved to the boy's room entrance, and watched the phone's screen for her to start moving again. There she was, and a moment later, he was out his door. He timed it so that he would pass by her as she entered the hallway just ahead of him. He said, "Hi, Sadey."

She looked startled. "You scared me, Des. Don't sneak up like that."

"Sorry," he said, not feeling sorry at all. He moved even closer as she headed toward her class. His hope was that they would "accidentally" bump one another. He loved it when she "elbowed him."

Des was suddenly overwhelmed. Her blood sang to him. Its attraction was so overpowering, he made himself pull farther away. It was either that or give in to the siren call of her pulsing arteries.

This was a rare moment when he briefly saw her as food, but he knew that sensation would quickly pass.

"See you at the dance," he said, veering off, and knowing from her e-mails that Conall might not go.

"Yes," she said.

If Conall did not attend the Sadie Hawkins event, Des would seize his opportunity. He was ecstatic.

2: VISITOR DES

*D*ES' ONGOING IMPRESSION WAS THAT Sadey hadn't heard from Conall lately. The guy hadn't been in school for the last two days. Maybe Des should call her again. She had not been answering lately, but she might change her mind now, about talking to Des.

He called her, and she answered on the third ring.

"Hello?" she said. "Des, what a *surprise.*"

He smiled. She had answered even though she knew it was him. He ignored her mocking stress on the word *surprise.*

He could not hide his happiness as he said, "Hi, Sadey. What're you doing?"

"I'm eating yogurt. How about you?"

"I haven't had my juice today," he said. "In fact, I was just thinking about having some yogurt. Yes, that sounds really good."

There was a long pause on her end. She seemed to be slurping her yogurt. Finally, she said, "Des, why don't you come over and visit me?"

"Okay!" he was taking no chance on her changing her mind. "I'll be right there."

"Do you know where I live?"

"Sure." He disconnected.

Des could also have added that he was out in front of her house calling from his cell phone, but he didn't. He simply walked to her front porch, and rang the doorbell.

In a minute, the door opened. Sadey got a shocked look on her face. It was as though she had expected someone else. "Des? How did you make it here so fast?"

"I was hungry for yogurt," he said, nodding at the cup in her hand.

"You know what I mean," she squeaked.

She did not look at all confident like she usually did at school. He thought she should be even more self-assured on her own turf. Never mind. He had to keep her talking and help her relax. He could not take a chance on her freaking out and sending him away. "Isn't technology wonderful?" he said, holding up his phone. "Aren't you going to invite me in...and close the door?"

"Sure, come on in," she said. "I'm just surprised how fast you got here."

He pushed the front door closed after him. "So," he said, "where's your bedroom?" After all, he reasoned, that would be her greatest comfort zone in the house.

"The *yogurt* is in the kitchen," she pointed the way.

"Oh, yes," he said, "we should probably eat first."

Sadey looked suddenly nervous, and he decided that he needed to choose his words more carefully. The truth was he had become overly excited. He noticed a bit of fresh color in her cheeks. She was feeling excitement as well—or was it fear?

The cell phone in her jeans waistband vibrated, and also rang.

Des looked down at the small white phone poking out the top of her pants. That was a strange, yet intriguing place to keep it.

She jumped, even though she had to know the phone was there. Maybe Des made her nervous. She pulled it out with lightning speed and flipped it open. "Hello?"

Des could hear a male voice, but not make out the words.

"Uh," Sadey stammered. She looked over at Des as if a thousand thoughts were flooding her mind.

Des believed he heard the other voice say, "Please." It was difficult to tell, because the word was spoken so softly.

"Sure, Conall, come right over." There was urgency in her voice.

This was the last thing Des wanted to hear. That creepy senior, Conall, had just ruined Des' whole day. Was she agreeing to this because she felt Conall's need was huge, or maybe she felt insecure being alone with Des?

He watched as Sadey slid her closed phone back into her waistband. She seemed distracted, perhaps by something Conall had said.

Des decided it was time to go. He moved closer to the door, and took hold of the handle.

Sadey noticed his movement, and looked surprised by his actions. "You just got here."

Des pulled the door open. "I'll visit some other time."

"What about the yogurt?" she asked.

"Conall can eat mine," he replied, as he disappeared through the entryway and closed the door behind him.

MOVING RAPIDLY DOWN THE STREET, he thought his scheme could not have turned out worse. What a waste. Now what would he do? Standing so close to Sadey in her own house had nearly set him on fire.

There had been no one else in her home. He could tell pretty accurately how many people were in a house when he entered it. His sense of smell was not as flawless as his mother's, but very good. There had, however, been a hamster present that was afraid, yet could not run and hide because it was in a cage.

He walked aimlessly at first, but then he decided to stop at the park along the river. Monmouth and Independence ran together like one big town, and he was now in Monmouth, beside highway 99W.

In the park, he found a shaded picnic table and sat down to make another call. He could hear the creek gurgling along through the park, and high-pitched laughter from some kids playing on the climbing structure.

"Hello, Amber," he said when he heard her answer.

"Hi, Des!"

She sounded thrilled to hear his voice. He was not so delighted by hearing hers, in fact, he was bored. He might as well create a second plan just in case things didn't work out between him and Sadey.

"What are you doing?" he asked her.

She groaned. "I'm babysitting. Boring! I'm so glad you called. This family does not believe in television. I bring my iPod even though they don't like me to, but I only put it on after the adults leave. The kids never hear it, anyways. What are you doing?"

"Calling you."

"I mean, what else? I hear screaming there. Are you babysitting, too?"

He thought for a moment before he told her where he was, feeling uncertain whether he wanted her to know his location.

"I'm in that park beside the highway, just when you enter Monmouth from the north," he explained.

"Oh." She sounded disappointed. "That is too far for me to bring the kids—too long of a walk."

That was the last thing he needed, for her to show up with a bunch of little snots. "No problem, we can just talk on the phone."

"Yes," she agreed. "Oh, are you coming to the dance?"

He had to be careful. Sadey was the one he wanted to dance with. He would have called and asked her, but it was a Sadie Hawkins event, so girls had to ask the boys.

"I might be able to," he said. "Although my parents want me to go to a concert in Portland that night." Those words were the actual truth, because it was to be a major hunting event, and full-sized family enterprise. Each of the three would play their part, although Boris would make the actual kill. Des and Natasha would help him separate one from the "herd," because young females seldom traveled alone.

"Oh." She sounded impressed. It did not take much to impress her, though.

"Have you ever done phone sex?" he asked her.

"Not really. Maybe a little bit."

He knew she hadn't. She might fabricate something though, and pretend she had. That would make things easier for him. "Are you comfortable?" he asked.

"Yes," she said, but there was a strain in her reply.

He smiled. "I want you to pretend we are kissing," he said. "Right now."

"Okay," she sounded more confident. Kissing was not such a threat.

"You can kiss the phone if you want," he suggested. "To make it seem more real." He guessed she probably would do that.

"Um-humh," she moaned softly.

Too bad she is not wealthy, he thought. He could probably sell her one of the big bridges in Portland, since she was that gullible.

"Let's pretend we have been French kissing for a while. You do Frenchies, don't you?"

"Of course," she replied.

Her response was so sudden, he thought he must have offended her by the suggestion she might not French kiss. "I knew you did," he said reassuringly. "Now, we are a little tired of that, and I am beginning to kiss along your jaw bone. Clear up to the nape of your neck."

He doubted she knew where her nape was, but she would be

afraid to ask. Now he would bait his trap.

"Then," he continued, "I start sucking on your ear lobe. Does that feel good?"

"Uh...huh."

"Great. Now I am sticking my tongue in your ear. Then...kissing your earlobe and sucking it again. Biting it ever so softly. Until it *almost* hurts. Then I pull on your earlobe with my teeth. Stretching it. Now I am sucking it again. Biting. Then sucking. Just imagine that for a while."

He gave her time to build on that image. "Now, I'm moving down your neck. I am kissing all the little ticklish spots. The ones that make you squirm with delight, and sending shivers through your body. Can you feel the goose bumps on your arms?"

He thought he heard her moan. He smiled. This was too easy.

"And now I'm sucking on your neck. I am moving around different places so I don't give you a hickey—yet. You've probably had hickeys before."

"Uh-huh," she cooed.

"I've found a spot on your neck. You love it when I suck there. Just imagine me sucking in that area for a time."

He definitely heard her moaning. Could he get her to bite herself, and suck her own blood? No, but he could probably talk her into doing this to someone else. Maybe he should just turn her, and use her for a vampire slave.

No. He must uphold his family tradition. His first time was definitely going to be a kill. It was a rite of passage, like an African tribesman bagging a lion—or something along that line.

Then he thought about Sadey. If he did this to Amber, Sadey would be next. He could not help himself. He probably did not stand a chance with her anyway, thanks to Conall. Oops, he stopped his wandering thoughts, better get back to Amber.

"Now, I am sucking on your neck so hard, you think you are going to die of ecstasy. I alternate with tiny little bites. Little love bites. It barely hurts at all. You do not want me to stop, it feels so good. In fact, you want—"

"Oh!" Amber groaned so loudly it hurt Des' sensitive ears. He pulled away from his phone. His suggestions must be really getting to her.

"I got to go," she said in a frantic voice. "The kids are tearing the kitchen all apart. Call me after I get home. Later—"

Right up until then, he'd had her.

The day was not going well for Des. Interruptions were ruining everything. In a bad mood, he looked around the park. There were three kids, and no parent in sight. His blood lust was high. First, he had been around Sadey, now he was all worked up from talking to Amber, and he needed an outlet.

He started toward the play structures. The two girls and a boy did not notice him. The oldest was no more than seven or eight. Des was halfway there when he spotted a dark head rise from a long tree shadow on the ground. A large German shepherd was eyeing him. Why hadn't he sensed the canine? The hairs were rising on the back of its neck.

That breed could be hard to deal with, especially in daylight, with witnesses. Des sniffed the breeze. The wind was from the west, behind him. That is why he still could not smell the dog. Drat. He turned and walked carefully away. He made it a point not to run, but he did not go in the opposite direction, just off at an angle.

When he glanced back, the children continued playing, and they were still unaware of his presence. The dog watched him with keen interest, though, because it probably sensed he was a vampire. Likely, it knew from instinct that if they fought, it would die. Still, it would sacrifice itself for the children. Des kept walking.

It was time to get home, anyway, and he was surprised his mother had not called to check up on him. Recently, she often worked late, so he would likely be eating dinner alone, and maybe he would actually drink his "juice" at supper. Although he'd sworn off being a vampire because he was going to quit for Sadey.

The whole quitting idea, however, was not working out. Life would be easier for him as a vampire. Besides, if he did not fulfill his established blood-sucking role, what would he do? He would be neither a human nor vampire, and most likely hated by both his kind and humans.

His mother was waiting when he walked in the door. Her nostrils flared. "You've been on the prowl, Desi. I love that smell about you. No kill yet, but you thought about it, didn't you?"

He nodded.

"Um," she said, "that girl you were with smells delicious. She is perfect for your first time."

He was not hungry, and went to his room without replying to Natasha.

3: ANOTHER ENCOUNTER

*A*T SCHOOL THE NEXT DAY, Des wondered why he had lowered himself to maneuver that pathetic girl, Amber. He knew she would do whatever he wanted. Certainly, her female fragrance was a major attraction. She definitely got his blood lust boiling, but that would ruin things for him and Sadey.

Once he went down the hunter's path, he would not be able to return to his current state. There would be no stopping after that. If he went through with killing Amber, Sadey would surely become his second victim. On the positive side, his parents would be proud.

There was one problem; he still didn't want to kill Sadey. His attraction to her was different, and stronger than anything—even sexual attraction, or blood-lust.

"Des," a feminine voice called from behind. "Wait up."

He wanted to ignore Amber. He could pretend he had not heard, but the memory of her scent stopped him. Des turned, watching her approach. He had wanted more of a challenge for his first time. She was so desperate for a boyfriend, she would do *anything.*

This would be pitifully easy, since he had set the stage with *phone sex.*

Out of breathe, Amber said, "Des, I'm so glad I caught you."

He knew she had that "I caught you" idea backwards.

"Let's skip first period," she said, "and find that quiet spot you told me about."

If he had any resolve left, it died when she got close to him. He took a deep breath, and she was heavenly. Her flavor would be perfect for his first conquest, and there was a lot to be said for that.

Long, involved "courtships of death" were surely overrated.

He thought, enough for outdated traditions. Grabbing her arm, he led her toward the shelter he had previously scouted out.

He felt her trembling, and inhaled deeply, savoring her aroma as he touched her soft skin. When they were nearly to his destination, he pulled her into a secluded nook, and took her in his arms. Why wait? Her books dropped on the floor, spilling out into the hall.

"Oh, Des," she whispered, as he sucked on her chin, moving toward her lips.

He stopped. They weren't in a secure location for what he planned to do. He strained to keep control—dared not kiss her neck because there would be no way to stop. Even with all his mother's efforts to desensitize him by making Des kiss her neck daily, he would bite at the first opportunity.

The bell rang, and Amber stiffened in his arms. "We better get out of here. Where is your hideout?"

He pulled her roughly after him. Her schoolbooks and binder remained on the floor but she didn't seem to notice, and he again knew she would do whatever he asked.

"You two are tardy," a man's authoritative voice announced behind them.

Something inside Des began to unravel. He must regain self-control or all would be lost. If he was not careful, he would kill them both, right there.

"Amber, are those your books on the floor?"

"Yes, Mr.—"

"Well, go and get them…and then proceed to class. *Now please.*"

She meekly obeyed without looking at Des, or the assistant principal, whose voice she had so obviously recognized. She simply walked away.

"You are new here," said the man, and Des nodded.

"I know you want to make friends. Nevertheless, this is not the way to go about it. I am cutting you some slack because you are new. What's your name?"

"Des Lugosi, Sir." The young vampire's words were soft, and smooth as velvet.

"Mr. Lugosi, I want you to go straight to class. Do not even think of having a tryst with that little girl on school grounds. Not now, or later. Do you understand?"

"Yes, sir." Des knew he could kill the man in thirty seconds or less. That was despite their size difference. It also took into account that the administrator was obviously a body builder. His physique had that characteristic, top-heavy shape.

Leaving the assistant principal—who stood there watching his departure—Des saw that Amber had gotten her things and disappeared. It was just as well. He might have used his persuasion on the administrator, but to what purpose?

T HAT AFTERNOON WHEN DES RETURNED home, his mother greeted him at the door.

He dutifully kissed her throat.

She purred, "Little Desi has found *her*, his first—the one. Um... she smells divine...good as the other girl."

So she approved of Amber. "I nearly did it," he said. "Almost got caught, too."

"Don't worry, dear," she said. "We can always move again if we have to. Your manhood comes first. You will remember forever your initiation, the first kill. Your lovely victim will be a part of you through eternity—in your memory." She sighed. "This is so perfect. I wish I could watch. Do you think you could videotape it?"

"And create the evidence the authorities would need to convict me? No way."

"Yes. You are right," she said. "Of course you won't do that. Do you plan to make love to her, too? Draw it out, and let her life linger, even as it ebbs?"

"I'm just going to do it, Natasha," he said. "Alright? Geez...."

"Males have no romance." His mother was disappointed, but left him alone.

He smiled. Maybe he *would* make his perfect moment linger.

"Have you been remembering to feed your pet?" she asked.

Des automatically held up the palm of his hand, revealing the most recent fang punctures, now almost completely healed over.

"Yeah," he said. Although having a vampire bat for a pet could literally be a pain.

4: DANCING DES

*D*ES GOT TO THE GYM EARLY, and stood off to one side, unnoticed. From his location, he could watch all the students enter the Sadie Hawkins dance. The large room began to fill, but most of the attendees stayed away from the middle of the floor. The Deejay was still setting up, running speaker wires, and checking his gear.

The assistant principal was highly visible, and Des also recognized a couple of teachers. Some music began, but only a few couples moved toward the center of the gym to dance. In the midst of all the milling around, Des spotted Amber. He would avoid her as long as possible. Then he noticed Sadey. Whoopee!

She was alone. Conall was nowhere in sight. Des took a circuitous path toward his goal. With Sadey near, he had no desire for Amber. The girls found each other, and stayed together, but he hoped someone would ask Amber to dance before he got near.

The gym lights darkened even more, and the flashing ball twirled high overhead. It was reminiscent of sixties-style disco, with strobe lights slashing through the semi-dark room. Despite some of the décor, the music was modern, and strongly vibrated the floor.

The energetic disc jockey announced the next song before the first had ended. When the new music began, he yelled through the microphone, "Get out there and dance! I wanna hear some foot-stompin' boys 'n girls."

Des was near his selected female by then, and Amber shouted something to Sadey, who looked in his direction. No use hanging back, he thought. Stopping near Sadey, just a foot away, he purposely invaded her space. In the dim light, he saw her staring at his green eyes. One girl had called them amazing. He smiled confidently.

Des reached out and took her elbow. He leaned in close to her ear, and said, "I would have called you, but it's a Sadie Hawkins."

She stared at him, not replying.

Then he realized, she probably assumed he was going to ask her to dance. "Oh, I'm sorry," he said. "I meant to ask. Would you like to dance?"

Without waiting for her reply, he led her to the boogieing area, and as they started up, he felt ever more confident. He was a great dancer—virtually professional caliber—and enjoyed the moment very much. When the dance ended, he took her arm and led her back toward Amber. Sadey had stiffened at first from his ongoing physical contact, but relaxed by the time they reached her friend.

Des released her arm. He did not wander off, however. Instead, he stood between Sadey and her BFF. After a moment, almost as an afterthought, he spoke to Amber. "Would *you* like to dance?"

She grabbed his hand, and dragged him to the very center of the gym. The spotlight that singled out couples immediately locked on them, and Des soon realized that Amber was born for the limelight, but then, so was he. Glancing over at Sadey, he was surprised that she appeared jealous. What wonderful news.

It was a slow dance and he pulled Amber in tighter. When he got a chance to look again, he could tell Sadey was definitely pissed. Since Conall had canceled, Des was, for tonight, the only guy paying any attention to the two girls.

The crowd blocked Des' view for a minute, and when he spotted Sadey again, she had turned away. Her body was stiff from the emotion of primitive negative energy.

At that same moment, a scream rose above the loud music. It came from Amber, who had yelled painfully in Des' ear. He looked about, trying to discover the reason for her outburst, but everywhere he gazed, dancers had stopped. The crowd parted, although Des could not see the reason. More importantly, Sadey was no longer visible and his ears were ringing.

With the crowd unnervingly silent, and most students looking toward the East end of the gym, nobody paid attention to the music anymore. The throng continued to separate, creating a funnel-shaped clearing. Des saw fear in peoples' eyes.

The teeming bodies parted even farther, with all attention focused along a vacant path running down the center of the floor. The music stopped, creating a powerful silence, and the DJ rose from his seat, craning his neck to see what was happening.

As Des visually followed where other's eyes focused, he saw a big lanky dog step into view. Moving first one way, and then the other, it occasionally sniffed the air. Des sampled the air as well—it was no dog. The animal was unkempt and shaggy, actually wild. Something in its eyes scared Des, yet fascinated him. In that moment, he knew it was a wolf.

The head roved from side-to-side until it caught a certain scent. In one bound, the great hairy beast landed in front of Amber and Des, who had already slipped behind her. He hoped the wolf would not spot him or catch his scent. Even so, this was no ordinary wolf—if there was such a thing.

It crouched low, and Des moved farther behind Amber, allowing her to face the wolf alone. It crept forward, preparing to leap, eyes locked on hers. Yet, Des knew it sought another. The beast was not searching for Amber, since it was really hunting him. It hunched lower.

Off to one side, out of fear for her friend, Sadey screamed, "No!"

The wolf turned and looked at her. In three bounds, it crossed the distance between Amber and Sadey. Des had seen the blood on its muzzle. He knew that even though it sought him, Sadey now looked death in the eye, and she could not breathe.

Still, Des did not move because self-preservation was more powerful in vampires than "normal" people. It had to be for them to survive. Des saw the terror in Sadey's eyes, yet he still did nothing. He couldn't afford to reveal his true nature in front of such a crowd. The wolf's stare never left her as the great beast moved slowly forward—one step, and a second—until it halted.

Another scream filled the gym. As the sound ended, Des knew it had come from Sadey. The wolf immediately turned and fled on silent feet. Loping past the onlookers, it disappeared from sight.

Sadey sagged to the floor, and Des moved swiftly, crouching beside her. He watched her eyes close, flutter...then remain shut. She was unconscious, but who wouldn't be? The damn thing had been terrifying.

5: DESTROYER DES

*D*ES HAD CAREFULLY PLANNED HIS special moment. Amber was such a fool to meet him alone in such a secluded woodlot. The cemetery was barely visible nearby, and empty as a vacant tomb. In his thoughts, their meeting symbolized the end of life—hers, anyway. The lonely graveyard would literally be Amber's last resting place. Perhaps he would prop her lifeless form against a tombstone. He smiled at the image in his mind, and enjoyed picturing her unseeing, lifeless eyes, set in her pale white skin.

She was certainly not dead, yet! When Des took her in his arms, she seemed aware only of her infatuation for him. She responded so completely, he felt mild guilt as he passionately kissed her. But he soon got over that. After all, she would be *his first.*

Des tilted her head to the side and pulled her hair back. She was so ripe, so ready. His mother's idea of making love the normal way, and culminating with the blood sucking—that was tempting. But he couldn't wait that long. Des would kill her with one long, delicious bite. Her ecstasy would be complete, though short-lived, and his would be absolute.

A familiar voice whispered a question. "Starting without me?"

Des looked up, not removing his lips from his victim's neck. This couldn't be occurring. Oblivious to the newcomer, Amber moaned with delight.

A male form moved nearer. Des could not believe the interruption of his *first time,* and by his own father. Des glared at the man who looked like an angelic teenage male.

"You must take your time," said his parent. "We can each nibble one tasty side of her neck."

Amber asked, "Who is this?" and pulled slightly away from Des.

"No one." Des hissed. He dared not proceed, because he could not safely take his eyes off his father.

"Is he a new student, too?" Amber sounded intrigued. "Does he want me?"

The handsome young man whispered, "Very much."

"They both want me," Amber whispered wistfully. It was every girl's dream come true. Two hot guys fighting it out to see which would win her.

A third streaking form appeared out of nowhere. When it stopped, there was a lovely teenage female. "Boris. What are you doing? It is little Desi's first time. Let him have his fun."

The two males paused in their conflict.

"He's ruining it," Des complained.

His father said, "He's botching the whole thing."

"Then let him," the girl-like mother replied. "You did the same with yours, if I recall correctly. Come home, *now.*"

To complicate matters even further, two more figures materialized beside Amber.

Sadey reached down and took Amber's arm, pulling her to her feet. "Come on."

Amber resisted.

"They are going to kill you," Conall said. "Come with us."

The three vampires stared at the newcomers. Des's father stepped forward, but his mother, Natasha, halted her youthful-looking partner. "No, Boris. You are coming with me. Our son can handle this. What a glorious thing. Imagine...a triple play for his first trophy hunt. He will be legendary!" She grabbed Boris' arm and whisked him away.

"You are ruining it." Amber shook free of Sadey. "Leave us. You are just jealous." Amber's anger at Sadey changed to confusion as Conall shapeshifted into an enormous wolf.

Two things surprised Des. He saw Conall change instantly into his wolf form, and in addition, his adversary was unbelievably quick.

Des, however, was faster. The problem was that the wolf seemed to anticipate Des' every move, managing to stay between the girls and him.

The vampire decided to harass the girls anyway. That would give the werewolf something more to worry about. Des flitted between trees and over uneven terrain so fast he was only a blur in the air. If he could cause Conall to lose sight of him for a couple of seconds, it would all be over. He would kill that little bitch, Amber. Then he would bite away at the demoralized wolf.

Amber yelled, "Stop! What is going on?" The last word had barely left her mouth when she simply disappeared.

Des had gotten closer, ready to make his kill run. He paused in confusion, losing focus. In that moment of slowed movement, the wolf attacked. It was nothing fancy. No slash at the jugular the vampire would have made. Instead, the gash at his ankle was meant to hamstring Des. The goal was to slow the quicker vampire down. Fortunately for Des, he was able to minimize the disabling cut through lightning fast reflexes. Still, he was injured.

Withdrawing a safe distance, he tried to make sense of what he had seen. Amber was there one second, protesting, and in the next moment she was gone. That made Des wonder about how Sadey and Conall had arrived in the first place. He'd previously assumed they had somehow snuck up. What if they'd just appeared? That was crazy.

Des realized the wolf was now behind him. Why had Des been so careless? He moved swiftly again, but this time Conall left a slice on his left thigh. Now he had cuts on both legs. As he zigzagged away, he saw the grass and bushes were smeared with blood. Surely that was not all his. Then he glimpsed the smudge-distorted air around the werewolf.

Boris and Natasha had returned, and Des was thankful. Despite his superior speed, he was not doing so well on his own. Anger that he needed saving caused Des to surge forward, straight toward Conall. He would teach the big mutt a lesson.

Too late, Des saw Sadey materialize just to the side, and slightly ahead of him. She pushed him hard, and Des was moving too fast to avoid her shove, which veered him straight into a solid oak tree.

That was the last he remembered, rocketing toward the large trunk. Seeing the fissures in the bark grow larger...and then— SMACK.

WHEN DES AWOKE, HE FOUND he was lying on the ground, and a tombstone stretched toward the sky above him. Large letters near its top proclaimed: REST IN PEACE.

On his chest was a sharpened wooden stake. It lay there innocently on top of his shirt, positioned above his heart, not pounded through his chest, as it might have been. The message was clear. Leave Sadey and Conall alone—perhaps Amber, too—or die.

Unbelievably, Boris and Natasha lay on either side of Des. They were still unconscious. He looked down at his legs. The gashes had stopped bleeding. Someone had tied a piece of his shirt around the deeper slice on his thigh. Sadey, he guessed. Conall would have just let him bleed to death, and Des could relate to doing that.

Where were the other two? Did they just disappear, only to materialize somewhere else? His parents had never told him about any such occurrences.

Des looked at his mother's features. Vampires healed quickly, almost miraculously, yet his mother's face was still swollen and discolored. Actually, her nose was broken and maybe her cheekbone as well. Her eyes blinked open as he stared at her face.

Natasha's left eye had a bloody streak across it. Internal hemorrhaging, he guessed. She looked awful. Not at all like the sweet young thing so many guys had given second appreciative looks at during visits to the mall.

She groaned, and tried to roll over, crying out in pain, and then laid herself back down, breathing with difficulty. Her wooden stake still rested between her breasts. She was definitely worse off than Des. He reached his hand out to comfort her, but she did not seem to notice.

Behind Des, Boris rolled on his side. He was quieter, but when Des turned to look, his father was obviously hurting as well. A bloodied bone splinter projected out of his shirtsleeve. Boris looked at the stake that had slid off his dad's chest into the grass when he repositioned himself. Boris picked it up. After studying it for a minute, he hurled it into the woods. "Ah!" he screamed, realizing for the first time how badly hurt he was.

It was a rude awakening, and Des decided that maybe they were not at the extreme top of the food chain after all.

6: DISASTER

DES AWOKE THE NEXT MORNING and lay in bed. He did not like to think about the previous day. Even so, he remembered limping home to get their van. He had driven it to the cemetery even though he did not have a license. Then he had helped his parents into the back—where they usually carried dead bodies. The irony was surely not lost on Natasha and Boris.

What would they do now? Des decided to hobble downstairs and see if his parents were up. Once he moved around, the stiffness lessened. He found the others in the kitchen, sitting at the table. It appeared he had interrupted a discussion, and there was an uncomfortable silence. Natasha's face looked much better, though unhappy.

Des got out a glass, and filled it with *water.* He was quite thirsty, but as he sat down with his parents, he felt their tension. He sipped his water, trying to sooth his scratchy throat. After a time, Boris broke the silence.

"We have to move," he said.

Des was not surprised. He nodded.

"However," Boris added, "you will remain here."

At first, Des did not know what his father meant. Des looked over at Natasha. She would not meet his eyes, and simply stared at the center of the table.

"We are nearly the last of the Old-line," she said in her middle-European accent that she usually tried to conceal. "We have disgraced our ancestors. We will begin again. Try to make things right. We will have another child, Boris and me. Perhaps this new one will…" Her voice broke, and she could not continue.

Boris added, "We are very disappointed in you, Des. We gave you every opportunity. Fed you the freshest, prime juice available. I taught you all I know about the hunt." His head lowered.

After a few minutes, Natasha left the room. Des knew she did not want to cry in front of them. It was very bad form in their exalted lineage. When she departed, something important left with her. She had always been there for Des.

His father spoke again, and Des wondered if Boris still considered Des his son, but he was afraid to ask.

"This house is paid for," Boris said. "You will have your cell phone if you need to reach us. Don't…unless it's an absolute emergency."

Boris's voice had also taken on Slovakian tones, and Des could not bear to look at his father's face.

"There is plenty money in the bank," Boris said. "You have debit card. Finish your schooling. Decide what you will be. Where you will go. Kill…or don't kill. It is your choice."

He stood and left.

Des felt like crying as the realization struck him. He was the most shamed, the most notorious failure in the history of his clan. Des was banished. It was similar to what some religious sects did— but they called it shunning. He was all alone.

There were various sounds in the house during the next hour. Then the front door closed very distinctly. Not slammed—but final. The van started up, and drove away.

Des was numb. He could not move for a very long time. He had the freedom he had always craved, but now he knew it was not what he had really wanted. If only he could go back and do things over. Make things turn out differently.

He felt a tear roll down his cheek as he wandered through the house. They had left the furniture. All the family pictures were still on the walls. It was as though they wanted to forget he'd ever existed by leaving all traces of him behind. Des had always felt like a stranger wherever they lived, because their family was so different. Now he felt empty. The aloneness was not something he could start to deal with yet. Des went upstairs, feeling the pain in his muscles like never before. In his room, he noticed that his pet vampire bat was gone, cage and all. Another loss, but not a big one. Des dropped on the bed. Maybe he could sleep.

DES HAD NO IDEA HOW long he napped, but a strange feeling passed through him. It was the sensation of motion. When he opened his eyes, he was not in his room. Not even in his house.

Looking around, he saw Sadey sitting on a bed. She was beside Conall, who lay there, obviously in worse shape than Des, or even his parents.

Where was Des, and how had he gotten there? He was so disoriented he wanted to throw up.

A moment later, Amber appeared out of thin air. She was bewildered, and collapsed on the floor.

"Time to talk," said Sadey.

Des glared at her. She was doing this to him. He knew she had somehow brought him there. More importantly, she was the root cause of all his problems, including his botched first kill, and abandonment by his parents. The list was long. She had ruined his life. Des would kill her if it was his last act on Earth. He crouched, ready to spring for her throat.

"Chill out," she said.

There was a brief sensation of motion before Des could see again. Barely an eye-blink later, he was in a frozen wasteland, with nothing but ice and more ice. The cold bit into his face, stiffened his lips, and he could barely breathe. The air hurt wherever it entered an orifice. His arms wrapped around his upper body of their own accord. He was literally beginning to freeze. Death was less than a few minutes away. He'd never really experienced cold before, certainly not in Western Oregon.

Des felt motion again, but assumed he was falling to the frozen ground to become part of it. A moment was required for him to realize he was back among the living. A voice spoke, and in another minute he recognized it was Sadey.

"I understand," she said, "that vampires don't feel the cold like the rest of us. The South Pole was just a hint of what I can do to you and your parents if you don't cooperate."

Des was still numb. His lips didn't work, but he did not want to go back to the cold, so he forced himself to speak. "What do you want?"

"We can't be friends, obviously," Sadey replied. She shifted position on the bed, taking hold of Conall's hand. "I want to make a deal with your family. You leave us alone, and that includes ungrateful Amber, here. In turn, we will leave you alone. Fair?"

Des remained silent. His body was adjusting to the warmer

room temperature. His mind struggled with the reality of her ultimatum. Was this the same girl he knew from before? The one he had been so smitten by that he'd lost everything?

"How long can you hold your breath? Sadey asked him.

What now? Des wondered, starting to worry.

"Do you deal well with lots of pressure? You know, the kind you will experience a mile under the ocean surface. Maybe pressure isn't your thing.

"The moon might be nice this time of year. No tourists. Only a little gravity. No oxygen to speak of, and the best part, from my view...no blood—except your own, as it freezes. I remember from science class that the dark side of the moon stays a couple of hundred degrees below zero. That was probably Fahrenheit, but it wouldn't matter much to you. You'd be dead before you really knew you were dying."

Afraid she might send him there for a sample visit, Des blurted, "Boris and Natasha have moved. They've left me here alone."

He saw a puzzled look on her face. Was it because he'd called his parents by their first names, or because they had abandoned him? Maybe she just didn't believe Des.

"Can you contact your folks?" asked Sadey.

He nodded.

"Let them know the deal we are willing to make. It is a one-time offer. The wooden stakes were a warning. I may be squeamish about pounding them through your black hearts, but I will have no trouble sending you away. Any place I select will not have a return flight."

"Okay," said Des. "I have nowhere else to go but here. The house is paid off, and they left me money. I'm not a successful vampire. I disgraced my family by botching my first kill."

He looked at Amber. "She was supposedly a sure thing."

"Fine," said Sadey. "We will talk to you in the school halls. You can even sit with us at lunch, occasionally. Just don't forget our treaty, ever—not even for a second."

"I won't."

Sadey smiled at Des.

He felt motion sickness again and found himself back in his room, where he collapsed on his rumpled sheets.

DES SPENT MANY HOURS IN his bed. He had no energy to do anything else. Most of his thoughts were bleak. His trip to the wasteland that was the South Pole still haunted him. Plus, there was the abandonment by his parents, and his lack of friends. All those taken together were overwhelming to his usually upbeat, and outgoing personality.

In addition, Des struggled with dietary concerns. He had always had an endless supply of human blood available, thanks to his parents. There were still vials in the refrigerator, but what would he do after they were used up? If he killed again and Sadey found out, that would be the end of him.

Before, when he was around Sadey, he did not want blood. He had poured it down the toilet. Now she did not want him near. How would he fight off his urge to kill? Could he survive on human food indefinitely? He had to face it, there was no real choice except to turn his back on his vampire heritage and traditions.

The final concern was other vampires. He was fair game now that his parents had given him up. He had always looked down on lesser clans, but without the support of his own lineage, he was at their mercy.

There was one final option. He could lure Amber for his first kill. Stockpile her blood and find a new home, far away, hoping Sadey did not catch up to him.

DES FORCED HIMSELF TO GO to school the next morning. He could not tolerate sitting home alone any longer. He rode the bus surrounded by noisy people, something he avoided when possible.

Walking through the school halls, he was extra alert because he wanted to see Sadey, Conall, or Amber before they spotted him. He would watch from a distance before he decided whether to approach one of them.

"Hi, Des," a girl said as she passed by.

He jumped before he realized it was not one of *the three*.

"Hi," he said after she was probably out of hearing. This was not like him. Get strong, he told himself.

Another girl said, "Hello."

He managed to answer in more reasonable time, and was surprised at how many kids smiled at him. He had friends at Centrist High, although he had never thought of them as such, since they had all been potential prey. He'd never really gotten to know any of them. Why become friends with one's food? It complicated things. His father had befriended a few humans, on occasion.

Des became fascinated at the positive responses he received

from other students. Preoccupied, he looked up to see Sadey thirty feet ahead, and moving right for him. She was on her cell phone and did not seem to see Des. He was certain she had, though. There was nothing he could do but keep going forward.

They passed without incident. Not even a sign of recognition.

He did not share any morning classes with Sadey, and it seemed Conall was not at school. That was a relief, but Amber was in Des' second period class. She was somewhat friendly, but did not come over to talk. They sat at the same table for lunch, but Sadey did not show up, and Conall was still gone.

Des soon realized the extent that Sadey had helped him avoid his vampire cravings. He did not know how she did it, and she probably didn't know either.

Amber sat across the table from him. She was chatty, as usual, but mostly to the girl beside her, Liz. Halfway through the mealtime, Amber briefly focused her attention on Des.

"You look lots better than Conall does," she said.

Turning to her female companion, she added, "They were fighting over me. You should have seen it. Almost scared me to death."

Des thought she *should* have been scared, but she was not wise enough to recognize how close she'd come to death.

"Conall got the worst of it, though," she turned back toward Des. "He's still home in bed. Sadey is eating lunch with him. She will be back in school afterward."

That meant Des would see her in class during the afternoon. That was reassuring. In contrast, Amber's incessant talk was painful, and repelled him, nevertheless, the scent of her begged him to—

"May I sit here?" A female voice said.

Des looked up. It was Dixie. She had said hello to him earlier in the hall.

"Dixie," Amber said too loudly. "Yes. Please do. You know Des."

Not as well as she would like to, Des thought. Nor as well as she ought to, or she would choose to sit elsewhere. He scooted over, allowing her plenty of room. For her part, she sat closer to him than she needed to, with her body touching him in the process.

"Excuse me," she said.

Des knew the physical contact was on purpose. "No problemo," he replied. He wiped his forehead with a paper napkin because he was starting to sweat. Female hormones surrounded him. Their body warmth spewed out aromas they could not imagine. He did not have to imagine, he knew their glorious scents all too well.

"Do you take Spanish?" Asked Dixie.

He replied, "Not this year. Last year, though."

"We have lots of Hispanic kids," she said, "but I think maybe Latino students is more politically correct now, it's hard to keep up. But anyway, there are plenty of chances to practice español, if you want."

She had no idea how right she was. It came in very handy in Salem malls for hunting Hispanic girls. He was also learning Russian. There were so many former Russians in Woodburn, and they often came to Salem to shop. Even so, Woodburn was less than an hour away. The Russian/Americans were easy targets if you learned the language and studied the culture. Not as easy as getting close to the Latinos, however, whose blood had more interesting flavor—from all the spices they ate, he guessed.

"Des is hot for Sadey," Amber said.

Dixie laughed. She was from the Deep South, and Dixie was her nickname.

Needing to change the topic, Des asked, "What part of Georgia are you from?"

"Ludowici," she replied, pronouncing the letter "C" like it was an "S." She added, "Down south, around Savannah...you'all." She laughed at her own exaggerated accent.

Des stood up. "I'm sorry but I have a test to study for." He left in a hurry.

7: TEST

DES ENTERED FOURTH PERIOD CLASS with some anxiety. The schedule changed every day, and sometimes fourth period came before lunch. Today, it was after. He was not supposed to be in this class, although Sadey was, and Conall would have been, except he was home recuperating. The only other choice for Des was to go home, a dismal alternative, at best.

He was currently supposed to be in a class with Amber, and since other girls were showing interest in Des, her attentiveness was resuming as well. So many girls were strange that way, as if they did not really have minds of their own. The temptation he felt near Amber was too great. He dared not be in the same room with her at the present time.

Sadey entered the classroom, and Des kept his head down. He had picked an empty seat to one side, and near the back of the class, hoping it was not assigned to anyone. Sadey did not seem to notice him. She sat near the front, which meant she was unlikely to look around. Des hunched down in his seat, just in case, and adjusted his head so the teacher could not see him well.

The blood lust had risen steadily in Des through his lunch break, but it soon leveled off just being in the same room with Sadey. What a relief. If only he could find something of hers to carry around with him—a small object that had the same effect on him as her presence, and capable of lowering his vampire thirst for blood. What was it about Sadey that reduced his desire for hunting human prey? He watched her out of the corner of his eye.

Dixie entered the room. Of all the bad luck, she *would* be in the same class as Sadey. Des lowered his head even more as Dixie sat two seats away from Sadey.

Right after roll call, the teacher said, "Clear your desks, but keep out a pencil. No talking during the test."

The blank exam paper sat on Des' desktop. He glanced over to see Sadey writing rapidly. He made sure the teacher could not see him, eased back even farther in his seat, got comfortable, and closed his eyes. He daydreamed about visiting Sadey. It was going well until Amber also visited her. He could not get away from that girl even in his imagination.

In disgust, he saw himself leaving Sadey's house. A long walk would relax him. Except, Amber followed Des, and she was beside him almost before he knew it. Her aroma sang mightily to his senses, so strong was her pull that he took her to the park by the highway where they wandered down by the woods. They were quickly seated in the grass by a tree, out of sight, and she was more willing than ever. Likewise, she was even more foolish than before. They kissed—French kissed, and he tried some things with his hands he had not done before. She did not stop him.

Des tipped Amber's head to the side, and pulled her hair away from her soft white neck. He wanted so much to bite, he could already taste her. She smiled, opened her eyes, and looked into his.

"Yes," she whispered. He bared his fangs. She nodded to go ahead. When he bit her neck, she moaned. This was what it was like.

"Des," it was Sadey's voice. "I warned you."

In horror, he opened his eyes. He was back at the South Pole. The frosty air bit into him. Except that this time, Amber was still with him, and Sadey, too. She said, "Chill out Dude."

When he looked at Amber, her neck was unmarked. The thought of what he had been doing to her revolted Des. He dropped to his knees and vomited. The contents from his stomach froze on contact with the air. It formed a mound on top of the layer of frost and ice that served as the ground.

Amber put her arms around him. She was soft and warm. He shivered against her. She kissed him. Her warmth melted the frost forming on his face. Her heat filled his whole body. He felt something different toward her, an arousal not driven by the desire for her blood. It was a strange and wonderful feeling. Des had a new inner drive. Similar to what he'd felt with her before, but more intense.

There was still a smile on his face when he opened his eyes and realized he was daydreaming. He was still in class, but the period had ended. The room was almost empty—just a few straggling students still filed out. Even the teacher had left.

Des exited the class, walked clear out through the front entrance of the school, and headed for home. He had to test this new sensation out. When he entered the front door of his house, he went straight to the kitchen. He opened the refrigerator door and removed a vial of blood. Its chill reminded him of his daydream about the frozen wastelands of the South Pole.

Des uncapped the vile. He brought the open top to his lips, and with a deep breath he inhaled the blood scent. It had no effect on him. There was no desire to ingest the liquid, so he moved to the sink and dumped it down the drain, feeling no remorse. It was an easy action that left him feeling guiltless. He did the same with all the other vials. At the last one, he paused. There was no turning back once he emptied it. The only other way to get blood would be to kill for it.

Des felt disoriented when Sadey appeared beside him. Was she a daydream or reality? He still held the container of "juice" above the drain. As Sadey watched, he poured it out. Then he rinsed the sink with water until all traces of red had disappeared.

"Are you okay?" she asked.

Des nodded.

"I felt you were there in class and looked over, but you seemed to be sleeping."

He just stared at her.

"Will you survive without that blood?"

He was not certain. "I think so. When I am around you, the need goes away. I don't know why. I wanted something of yours to keep with me, thinking that would help me not mess up when you aren't around. That's when I had the daydream."

Des stopped. He reached out slowly and touched Sadey's arm, just to be sure. "I wanted to check...to be certain...you might have still been my daydream."

His reverie had felt too real—the frozen ground, Amber's warm kiss. So, how was he to know what was real?

Sadey patted his arm reassuringly. "Let's talk." She led the way to the living room, and sat on the couch. Des followed, sitting well away from her. His blood lust seemed to be gone, but he would take no chances. The two of them were alone in his house, and things could get out of hand. He did not want to experience the cold again.

"Your parents are gone?" she asked.

"Yes, but I don't know where." Des said. "They told me not to contact them. But I still have my cell phone." He struggled not to cry. His lineage never cried.

Sadey said, "You sat by Amber at lunch today." It was not a question. She knew he had.

He nodded. "She was across the table, and Dixie sat beside me."

"How did that go?"

"I wanted to suck their blood. Something about Amber stirs me up. Dixie sat so close, her body touched mine." He shivered at the thought. "That is why I went to your class. I was afraid to be in the same room with Amber. Then Dixie came and sat by you. That is when I started daydreaming."

"Do you want to bite me, too?" she asked.

He hesitated. "I never have wanted to bite you. When we are together there is something different I don't understand. If only it would last. I think the daydream changed me permanently, though."

"I hated you," Sadey said. "For what you did to Conall. For what you were about to do to Amber. Conall is still weak. If you hurt him again, I will kill you. When I am around you, though, the hatred goes away. I have no idea why."

Des stared at her. He could see she wanted to hate him. Somehow, there was a peculiar kinship between them. A strange bond neither could control.

"I am all alone now," he said. "It is difficult for me. I don't fit into the vampire world...or with humans. Without the protection of my family, other vampire clans may kill me. I have no one, and nowhere to go. I stay close to you so I do not kill humans. So far, I have not murdered. I did go with Boris when he killed, though. Many times."

Des looked over toward the sink, and realized the last vial he'd emptied was from their final victim in Salem. She'd died for nothing. Her essence was wasted—poured down the drain.

"You knew which people's blood was in each vial?"

"Yes." It was family pride to know that. We could savor a particular essence, like sampling a rare wine. Tonight we'll have...."

She shuddered. "Oh, God save me! You are monsters. Why do I feel the need to help you?"

He shook his head. He had no idea. When he was with her, he partially connected with the heart of her revulsion. He could almost get in touch with her general caring for people, and move past his belief that they were simply food.

Sadey disappeared. He was alone on the couch. She was the

only person who really knew and understood who he was. She could not accept it though.

She returned, and there was a tear down her cheek. "Something I can't understand always makes me come back. I hate that more than I loathe you."

She stood and walked aimlessly around the room. Warning him to, "Stay on the sofa."

Sadey finally stopped and looked at him. "These are the rules. You will follow them, or...just follow them. All right?"

He nodded.

"You can sit at my table every day at lunch, but not right beside me. Down at the end, maybe.

"Amber still does not get it that you were going to kill her. You and I will meet with Amber, and you will tell her everything. You will say what you are. What you wanted to do...and nearly did to her. She has to understand. She must leave you alone."

"Yes," he agreed. Inside, he cringed. Secrecy was everything. Never telling about who he was to someone ordinary.

Amber appeared at the other end of the Davenport from Des, looking disoriented.

"Tell her," Sadey commanded.

"I'm a vampire," Des informed her. "I was going to suck your blood and leave your lifeless body lying in the cemetery. You were to be my first kill. My mother wanted me to make love with you first. It would have been a dual decimation, ending with my fangs in your neck. Biting your jugular would have happened while we...." he trailed off. "You get the general idea." He turned to gaze at Sadey.

She stared at him. What he had just said hit her hard.

He saw in her eyes that she forced herself to remain in the room. She had resolved to carry out her plan to the finish.

"Tell her everything," Sadey ordered.

"Amber, I never liked you as a girl, only as a food source. Well, it was special that you would be my first kill—kind of a rite of passage—earning my manhood. Like some guys go out and shoot a deer or an elk.

"We bite, and suck, and kill. It is the thrill of the hunt, but also for our food, and our way of life. It is my heritage, but I have stopped. My parents have abandoned me. They've left.

"Even so," he continued, "you should never trust me. We should not ever be alone together. You should not fantasize or romanticize about what that would be like. It is certain death for you. Your life will be down the drain, no happily ever after. No family and kids, just dead and gone."

Amber cried. "I thought you cared about me."

"No. Only as food, or as my first kill. You were never anything more to me. I didn't have any of the feelings you imagine—the emotions *you* have. The only things I cared about were me and my family. Our way of life: heritage and traditions."

Sadey said, "Amber, tell no one about this. If you do, like I said before, I will send you away permanently. Des is trying to change. He needs our help. In your case, that means not throwing yourself at him. Steer Dixie away from him, too. Do not tell her why, but just help her find another guy to be interested in. Understand?"

Amber's head bobbed up and down. Tears bathed her face, and she sniffled as she wiped her nose.

After Amber dried her face with a tissue, Sadey said, "You are going home now," and Amber disappeared.

Sadey said, "Des, call me if you want to bite someone."

Then she vanished.

8: VISITING CONALL

SADEY STOOD BEFORE DES WITH a stern look on her face. "We are going—end of story."

He didn't really want to. He and Conall were enemies, even with the "treaty." But he decided it was best to go at night, since he had more energy then. It was nearly eleven P.M. and Sadey had gotten real bossy. He didn't like that about her, and yet he said, "Okay."

He was still finishing the word *okay* when they arrived in Conall's bedroom. Des thought it was lucky for Conall that the shapeshifter was fully clothed. Did Sadey check those things out, or just show up? If she did pre-visits, she probably saw plenty. Funny, Des never used to think like that before. He had never cared much about human bodies, naked or clothed, except for supplying blood.

Conall did not have to say so, but it was obvious he was not pleased to have Des in his house. His nightstand lamp cast yellow light across the room.

"You both agreed," Sadey said, using a stern voice.

Des thought Conall looked somewhat better than the last time he'd seen him. Apparently, werewolves healed faster than normal humans, too. Conall's currently un-bandaged wounds were still rough and red.

"I'm starting to figure all of this out," Sadey declared. "We have to work together, and we must get over our negative feelings about one another."

"Together for what?" Des asked.

"I'll get to that. Think about this for right now. Before I did my magic with Conall present, it always turned out wrong. He thought he might possibly be a werewolf, but he couldn't remember what happened. And you, Des, were never meant to be a vampire. Together, we are something much better than we were separately."

Des was not convinced. He moved around uneasily, thinking about his life. No parents, no friends.

"I don't believe I have it better," he said.

"You have new possibilities," Sadey said. "So do Conall and I. My magic always turned out wrong. Conall was a slave to moon phases, dreading each new month. You, Des, were going to be a vampire for the rest of your life, feeding off others. Once you killed Amber, your fate would have been determined and you could never alter it. We have all changed our destinies.

Conall sat up in bed.

Des viewed him closely, whispering, "What is going on here?"

Conall's raw red wounds, from only a moment before, were now soft pink, with new tissue. His skin was smooth, and there were no telltale indentations where deep gashes had been earlier.

The werewolf boy got out of bed. He stretched his arms back, and his muscles rippled. "I'm hungry," he said.

"Well, don't look at me," Des replied.

Sadey seemed surprised at the change, but said nothing. She simply kept watching.

Conall left for his kitchen. He came back moments later with an overflowing sandwich. "There's more in the fridge, if you guys want some." He began devouring his food.

A moment later, he stopped, and swallowed his current mouthful, asking, "Who are those kids over on the corner?"

When Conall said that, Des had an uneasy feeling. He went to the window, but he could not see the street-crossing from there.

"Try the bathroom," Conall said, and took another bite.

Des went down the hall and found the restroom. He left the light off, and slid the frosted glass slider open a couple of inches, and then a couple more. There they were, five of them standing under the streetlamp. It was a pole light with the strange amber hue that doesn't show things very well. Still, he recognized the group immediately with his night vision, which was superior to most people's day vision. He clearly made out the features of the scruffy Portland vampires he'd seen at the Lloyd's Center ice rink. His parents had not even nodded at them. Undoubtedly, all five were on the hunt for Des, and they were obviously watching Conall's house.

As Des continued to observe, he saw Amber coming down the

street. No way! This could not be happening. He thought of Conall's room—and he was there. That had never occurred before. Perhaps Sadey had brought him.

"Vampires," he said. "Amber is heading right for them."

He pictured a spot between the gang and her—and immediately stood at that location. Amber was clueless as always. What was she doing walking along the street that time of night?

"Hi, Des," she said. "Are you going to Conall's too?"

"You should not be here," Des warned her.

She walked right up to him. "I'm not afraid of you, Des. I have every right to visit my friends if I want to."

He smelled her aroma, but it did not excite him the way it had in the past. He turned his head. The leader of the five ambled closer.

"How nice," the leader said, "a midnight snack." He was dressed in black, except for his soiled white t-shirt. He wore a nose ring pierced through the tissue dividing his nostrils, and large enough that Des wondered if it didn't get in the way when biting someone.

Amber seemed to notice the others for the first time. "I'm not afraid of you guys." She pulled out her cell phone. "I'll just call 911."

"Ooh, we're scared," the leader said, now only fifteen feet away.

His companions laughed.

Des said to her, "Cops would never get here in time." He faced his opponent, who stopped.

The lead vampire said to Des, "Better run home to mommy and daddy." The mocking tone suggested they knew he no longer had his parents for protection.

"You guys are a long way from home," Des said.

"Who are they?" Amber asked.

"Yes," said the nearest one. "Tell her who we are."

By then, the other four had moved up behind their leader.

"Like me," said Des. "They're vampires. Only they're the lowborn type."

Amber was not self-confident any longer. She hid behind Des, clutching her phone. The truth was, Des had never been in a real fight with another vampire. Let alone, five at once. Those guys were street-smart. He looked closer. Two were females, but with their baggy dark clothes and hair cut short, it was hard to tell.

That made it an even worse situation, because females tended to rely more on cunning than brute force. He had no sooner thought that, when he noticed them separating from the three guys. The girls whispered together, and then distanced even more from each other, moving to flank Des on either side. He knew they would attack simultaneously, without warning.

It looked like his only choice would be to grab Amber and try to outrun the five. There was not much chance of that, however.

Sadey appeared right in front of one girl, who stopped. There was a startled look on her face, and Sadey said to her, "Need a light?" In her right hand, she held a lighter, which she flicked open, placing her thumb on the spark wheel. In the other hand, she held a spray can of something apparently quite flammable. "I'd love to share," Sadey said.

She flicked the lighter and it flared as she pushed the propellant's spray button. The result was a miniature flamethrower. Not too mini, however, as the flame seared the she-vampire's face, singing her eyebrows and hair. Her heavily mascaraed eyelashes completely disappeared, and her nose looked badly sunburned to the acute eyes of another vampire such as Des.

Before there was time for the vampires to react, Sadey appeared in front of the other female, and did an instant replay, without the friendly chatter. Then she was gone. Leaving both vampires disfigured. They shrank back, even though their enemy had vanished.

The element of surprise was gone, and the three male vampires crouched to spring. They did not see Sadey, and then Amber, materializing behind them. They also didn't notice a streaking wolf dart from the shadows at one side. He approached at incredible speed, and before they knew he was there, he had already passed by, leaving deep gashes in all three vampire's lower calves.

Des took that as his cue to move. He darted to the nearest female and grabbed both of her arms. Swinging her around as if she were a doll, he flung her into her counterpart twenty feet away. While those two fought each other, crazed by their painful burns, Des leaped again.

The male vampires were checking out their deep wounds. They had each turned half around, trying to determine what was happening to them. Des grabbed the leader by his uninjured leg, and swung him like a strange baseball bat, knocking his head into the other two. The sound was like a ripe melon hitting a concrete floor.

Continuing to swing the leader, Des made another half circle before launching him discus-like in the air. The surprised vampire sailed a quarter of a block, where he landed headfirst on the pavement, which sounded even worse than the smashed melon noise.

Without stopping, Des made a similar move on a second male vampire, launching him in the other direction, which also ended in a sickening thud. The third fellow tried to run, but his leg was so badly injured, he was easily caught and launched almost straight upwards.

Des warned, "Incoming!" and all but the two female vampires moved away to safety before the inevitable splat on pavement.

Des approached the she-vampires where they lay in a cluster of arms and legs after having clawed and bitten each other mercilessly.

He said, "Clean-up on aisle one," followed by, "better bring the torch, Sadey."

She yelled, "Coming," while the two vampires scrambled away as quickly as possible.

Des easily caught up with first one, and then the other, dragging them beside an unconscious male vampire.

"When I said clean-up," he said, "I meant you two will do the cleaning up. Take these three guys with you. Don't ever come back. If I see any of you again, you will regret it. In fact, it will be the last thing any of you ever remembers.

"I'm coming back in a half-hour to check things out. There better be none of you left here, and nothing out of place."

*H*AVING RETURNED TO CONALL'S HOME, Des noticed Amber looking back-and-forth between the others as they sat in the werewolf's bedroom. It was as though she finally understood they were all *really* different.

"Thanks for your help," Des said to Sadey and Conall.

Sadey replied, "It was sort of fun. I've always loved fireworks."

Amber laughed loudly at her friend's remark. However, it was a strained, high-pitched laugh full of tension. Des thought she might be near to an emotional crack-up.

"Maybe you should lie down, Amber," he said. "We'll make room for you." He started to rise from the bed.

"No, I'm fine." She'd sat backwards in her seat so the backrest was in front, and she clung onto that. "You guys were awesome."

"More like, gruesome," Conall said.

It was at that moment, Des realized the werewolf had turned back into a human in less than a minute. By the time they'd entered his front yard, Conall had looked normal. But how he'd become fully clothed, Des had no clue.

Des said to Sadey, "I'm sure glad you moved Amber over by you. I was worried they would separate her from me, and that would be the...." He looked at Amber. Then decided not to say she would have been dead. Instead, he added, "That would've been bad."

Sadey glanced at Amber and then said to Des. "*I didn't move her...I swear.*"

"You had to..." he began.

Amber's voice was so soft it was barely audible. "I wanted to be with my friend."

Des thought about her words. What exactly did they mean? He asked, "So?"

"I moved," Amber answered.

Sadey studied her friend. "You teleported...like I do?"

"Uh-huh." Amber agreed.

"No," Des said. "That's not possible."

Amber disappeared from the chair where she was sitting, instantly materializing before him, her face inches from his. "Why?" she asked. "Amber can do it. Why can't I?"

"She's a witch," he explained. "Besides...there is no way four people who just happen to know each other—"

Sadey cut him off. "Maybe none of it was a coincidence. I've had a feeling about this for a while. I think we were all drawn together for a purpose."

"We were," Amber said. There was assurance in her tone for the first time. "I'm the Way-Giver."

"The what?" Des asked.

"The one who will know when we are supposed to do something important—together. And what that something is."

Conall spoke for the first time. "This is making my pores itch. Next, I'll be a wolf again."

"No," said Amber with complete assurance. "The time is not yet. But soon...."

She stared into Des' eyes. "I am not afraid of you, because none of you can ever hurt me. I am your Way-Giver. Without me, you will all drift aimlessly. Without Sadey, you three could not be together. You and Conall would kill each other. But if I weren't here, you would have no purpose. I bring the knowledge. Not all at once. Just one piece at a time. "Like this..." she leaned forward and kissed Des with her soft warm lips.

That warmth built within him. It raced through his veins, stirring something he had not previously felt. When he smelled her essence, it did not bring blood-lust.

Although none of it could make logical sense, Des knew that what she had said was the truth.

Unbelievable as it seemed, Amber was their Way-Giver. But shouldn't Sadey be the Way-Giver? She was so much more powerful and capable, in every way. Amber, on the other hand, seemed like a total loser.

THE END

(Of Book II of W.V.W. Trilogy, turn a page for Book 3)

BOOK THREE

WITCHERY
INDEPENDENCE

1: WITCH & WAY-GIVER
—BEGINS: *AFTER* Sadie Hawkins Dance—

*S*ADEY LAY SPRAWLED OUT ON her bed. She was watching her best female friend Amber, reflected in the mirror above the dresser. Amber was attempting a hair makeover. She had invited Amber to spend the night, and it was already dark outside.

Sadey was attempting to make sense out of things that had happened the previous evening. Finally, she asked Amber, "What did you mean by 'Way-Giver?' You said you are the *Way-Giver*. Will you explain that to me?"

"You brought the four of us together," Amber said, "but I'm the one who will know what happens next, when we are needed... and where. I'll tell you if we are required for an important..." She struggled to find a word.

"Mission?" Sadey offered.

"Yeah...sort of. I do not know how to explain it. I will hear the call to action, and tell you three what is to happen next."

Sadey thought that was part of *her* job. Until last night, she'd viewed Amber as a liability, a friend Sadey had to protect from her own foolishness, because Amber was the girl most likely to be eaten alive by a vampire—namely, Des.

"Just the day before yesterday," Sadey said, "you didn't believe I was a witch. And you thought Conall wasn't really a werewolf, although you had seen him turn into one to defend you from three vampires—including Des."

Sadey continued, "When Conall and I arrived to save you, Des' fangs were an inch from your jugular. He had lured you over by that old cemetery...remember? And when his father showed up, they fought over who would bite your neck."

Amber said wistfully, "They both wanted me."

"To kill you! Suck your veins dry." Sadey couldn't believe Amber was so clueless. For Heaven's sake, Amber was Sadey's age—fifteen years old. She made good grades in school, and *seemed* intelligent.

"Come over here," Sadey demanded.

Amber complained, "But I'm doing my hair."

"Do it later. I need you here...*right now.*"

Amber dropped her hair with an exaggerated sigh, and minced across the room. She threw herself on the bed. "Now what?"

Sadey took Amber's head in her hands and stared into her eyes. "This is what Des told you: 'Amber, I never liked you as a girl. Only as food...it was special that you would be my first kill, kind of a rite of passage. You know, earning my manhood.'

"He didn't care about you, Amber. He still doesn't, and told you never to trust him. How much plainer can he make it for you?"

What Sadey had told her friend was true, but there was a secret she'd kept to herself: her unreasoning crush on Des. But anyway, if Amber was a real friend, she wouldn't have gotten in Sadey's way.

"People change," Amber said.

In exasperation, Sadey shouted, "Not you!" She let go of Amber's face, mumbling, "I give up."

"Are you mad at me?" asked Amber.

Sadey rolled her eyes, and turned over onto her back, staring at the ceiling. "I'm way beyond mad. More like furious. Des told me you were such an easy victim it was *pathetic*. He almost decided not to kill you because there was no sport in it. But his folks were going to make him do it anyway."

Amber nodded her head, and started to cry. She moaned, "It's too awful. I can't deal with it...all right?"

Sadey realized that *she* was the clueless one. While growing up, Sadey had many signs telling her she was a witch. She'd tried to ignore them because she simply could not be a witch. It had taken years for her to accept the truth.

Conall's experience was similar. He knew he always blacked-out at the time of a full moon. He'd worried that he might be a werewolf, but had denied it until recently.

Why should Amber be any different? How could she immediately accept as fact what Sadey and Conall had struggled to understand for years?

Sadey took a deep breath, and let it out slowly. "Okay, Amber. Let's drop this topic—for now. What do *you* want us to do together? I mean it...whatever you want, that's what we'll do."

"Really?"

"Yes."

"Will you help me with my hair?" The look on Amber's face suggested she did not expect Sadey to go along with the idea. Sadey knew that Amber hated her naturally curly hair, and said, "Why don't we just straighten it?"

"Yes! I would love that, only..." she looked at the nightstand. "I don't think we have time. Answer your phone."

Sadey said, "What?"

At that moment, her cell phone rang.

Sadey grabbed her mobile off the nightstand, and put it on speakerphone. "Hello," she said.

Conall's voice sounded as if he was panicking. "I'm starting to turn. Why is that? How come you didn't bring me with you?"

Amber yelled, "Des is in trouble. We must help...!"

She disappeared.

"Great," Sadey said, "our Way-Giver just..." she changed her mind. There was no time for mean words. She had to get to her friend before he shape-shifted.

Conall sounded frantic, "Amber just what?"

"Nothing. Are you home?" Sadey asked,

"Yes," he growled.

She appeared in his bedroom in time to see his final transition into full wolf form. He began pacing the room in long strides, his shaggy head swaying from side to side.

Sadey went over and pulled down his window blind just to be sure no one outside could see him. "I'm going to check out Des' place," she told her werewolf friend. "Don't leave. I'll be right back."

She found Des' bedroom empty. The vampire could be anywhere. She began flitting from room to room through his house. No sign of Des.

When she appeared out in his yard, the scene was far from empty. A gang made up mostly of white guys milled around the night-shrouded neighborhood. Sadey activated her night vision. She saw they had especially long eyeteeth visible even though their mouths remained closed. None smiled.

Heads turned immediately as Sadey materialized. She felt like a plump hen sitting in the middle of a fox's lair—a den overly filled with hungry foxes, all of them ready to spring.

Des whispered from beneath his front porch, "Under here."

There were so many vampires watching, and their night vision was probably better than hers. Therefore, Sadey decided to confuse them a little bit. She appeared in front of a group of three males standing down the block. "You are kind of hot," she said to the middle one, "but what happened to your fang?"

Somehow, his right canine tooth had been mostly broken off. "You might want to see a dentist," she said. "We have a couple of good ones right here in town."

Before they got over their amazement, Sadey disappeared. She and Des materialized in Conall's bedroom, where he was still pacing. A moment later, Amber joined them. Her arms were full of small spray bottles.

She said with enthusiasm, "Cold pressed garlic oil. One thousand squirts per bottle. Each bottle equals 150 cloves. Sorry it took so long, I had to find enough money to pay for all this. I couldn't just steal the stuff."

Sadey was furious. "Garlic doesn't work on vampires," she said. "And you went off without telling me where Des was."

"He was *at home,*" Amber said, as though everyone should have known that.

Des took one of the garlic containers from his *friend* and read the label. "This does not work on my family, but we are different from most vampires. I wonder..."

Sadey grabbed a bottle as well. "Be right back." She disappeared.

She rematerialized, sitting on Des' rooftop, because she didn't want to take a chance on appearing too near—or on top of—a vampire who might be wandering around the street. The three she had visited earlier were now closer to the house. She showed up just behind them after removing the cellophane wrapper from the garlic container. "Hi again," she called out in a cheery voice.

Startled, the three began to turn around and Sadey sent three well-aimed squirts of concentrated garlic juice into their faces. She immediately returned to the rooftop to watch the results, which were dramatic. The trio of vampires fell to the ground, thrashing about. Their faces were contorted so strongly, she could see some of their reactions clear up on the roof. The vampires raked their faces with their hands in futile attempts to remove the garlic oil.

Sadey was not the only one viewing their reaction to garlic. The other alarmed vampires looked around warily for the source, and their frantic activities were like a hive of disturbed hornets.

Amber spoke from behind Sadey, "It looks like they will be ready for you next time. Better be careful."

Sadey nodded without responding. Her mind was already dealing with the new variable. "Stay alert," she told Amber just before disappearing from the roof's peak.

In the basement of her own home, she soon located what she sought, a little-used, highly pressurized squirt gun resembling a plastic rifle with a two-liter soda bottle on the top. During her return trip, she made another stop for more garlic, which she put in the squirt gun. Topping it off with water to make a fifty-percent solution, she returned to the roof where Amber was still sitting.

The vampires had decided to gather in a single group, giving aid to the three downed members, and forming a more difficult target for their opponent—they thought.

In quick succession, Sadey appeared seventy-five feet to the side of the gathering, firing a machine-gun-like sweeping blast before she disappeared.

She materialized at a similar distance from another direction, shooting a second sweep of the deadly spray. By then, she'd downed a number of vampires, all writhing in the street.

Returning to Amber on the roof, she warned, "They are desperate. If they spot you, disappear and go home."

Before Amber could respond, she and Sadey witnessed the form of a streaking wolf as it cut through the vampires like a predator in a slow-moving herd of cattle. He mostly clipped at leg tendons, avoiding their upper bodies and deadly fangs.

Sadey noticed the original five gathered in a little group at the center of the mass of vampires. As yet, they had been untouched by the garlic or the wolf. She thought of an idea that seemed like it should work, but if it didn't, she could be in mortal danger.

Appearing fifty feet in the air above the five, she fired a strong blast downward as she began to fall. She twisted the spray gun so that its deadly concoction completely covered her selected victims. Then she vanished by the time she reached a distance of fifteen feet above their heads. Back on the roof, she heard Amber say, "That was awesome."

Sadey smiled. Yes it was. And yet, she had regrets about the obvious pain she was inflicting on other beings.

Movement inside the disrupted mob of vampires drew Sadey's eye. It was barely a streak through the air until it paused. Des crouched above the wriggling form of one of the original five—a male. Holding a sharp wooden stake to the vampire's chest, Des pounded it in with a mallet. Then he was gone.

Sadey willed herself to see more clearly, and her eyes went into zoom-viewing mode. She immediately wished she hadn't. The vampire's back arched above the pavement, and a black fluid spurted out around the stake. His limbs flailed and he screeched in death's agony. Something like dark liquid fire seemed to consume his form, moving outward from the stake, devouring all the flesh and bones, leaving only a murky puddle trickling along the street surface. The stake floated on it briefly, and then settled to the asphalt.

 In rapid succession, the remaining four suffered the identical fate. Des reused that same stake until they had all been dissolved, and then he halted in front of the surviving group of vampires.

"They were warned," he said, "and now you are warned...."

"Leave here. Don't ever come back. Never track me or my friends...or your fate will be just like..." he pointed to the dark spots on the pavement, "theirs."

Still pointing to the moist discolorations on the street, he said, "We could easily kill all of you right now. In the future, we will not show mercy."

None of the onlookers replied. Most suffered from the effects of garlic juice. Some looked questioningly around at the others in their group, as if for direction.

Des became impatient. "Be gone...now!" he yelled. In a quieter voice he added, "Or die." His green eyes eagerly sought any who might oppose him.

In moments, the vampire assembly had dispersed and fled.

2: THE MISSION

SADEY GATHERED THE FOUR ALLIES together in Des' house. By then, it was after midnight, but Des had no parents at home to ask questions.

Sadey said to her companions, "Do you guys think the vampires will return?"

"Not for a while, at least," Des replied. "Most won't ever try a rematch, but a few may eventually decide to come back."

Conall had again converted to human form. "We will kill any who do, though, that's for sure."

Des nodded agreement.

"The garlic worked well, I thought," said Amber.

"My whole neighborhood smells of garlic," Des said.

Conall quipped, "I call that an improvement."

"We showed what we can do," said Amber, obviously trying to keep peace between the two rivals.

"There were some glitches," Sadey said. "But I think we can learn from those and do better next time." She decided not to question Amber about her initial disappearance. It was important to build on their strengths, and generate team spirit.

Sadey's cell phone rang. She realized it had been tucked in her waistband through the entire vampire ordeal. Amazingly, it had not fallen out. She didn't recognize the caller's number. "Hello?"

A male said, "Congratulations on winning your little skirmish."

"What?" Sadey asked. She wondered who the guy talking to her could be.

"I'm James Joyce, an old friend of Conall's."

Sadey activated the speakerphone. "Do you want to talk to Conall, Mr....uh...Joyce, was it?" Then she wondered why he'd called *her*. "How did you get my number?"

"That is not important," he replied. "The significant thing is that you survived your little vampire quarrel. Let's call it a test...and now you are ready for an actual assignment."

"Who are you?" Sadey asked.

"You may call me James Joyce, if you wish. My real identity must remain hidden. Think of me as a special sort of *Charlie* and yourselves as my angels." He gave a little laugh. "Yes, you can call me Charlie if you want to."

Conall said, "Are you the comic book guy? The one who called me a couple of weeks ago?"

"The very same," answered the male voice. "Of course, I wasn't really interested in you as an illustrator. I wanted to know more about you as a werewolf."

"Illustrator?" Sadey said, looking quizzically at Conall.

"Never mind," the voice continued. "Now it is time for your real mission. I need for you three—"

Sadey said, "There are four of us."

"Not really. Amber is just a little tag-along. She isn't part of our actual team."

"*Our* team?" Des asked.

"None of you are really the mastermind type, are you?" the voice said. "You need me to orchestrate your...."

Conall tried to pull the phone from Sadey's hand. There was anger in his eyes.

She managed to keep hold of her phone, and moved it closer to her face. "No thanks, Mr. whoever you are." She ended the call.

Sadey looked over at Amber. There was more hurt in her friend's eyes than she had ever seen there before. Amber couldn't look at any of the others, and Sadey knew that her friend had struggled to assert herself in their group. She'd tried especially hard for Sadey to take her seriously. Then, to have some random adult say with authority that she was nothing but a tag-along had been too much for her.

Something then changed in Amber's eyes. It was as if she had suddenly been inspired. Looking at Sadey, she said, "I know who that guy is...and what he's up to. He is our *archenemy*. His mind is so black that a thousand vampires after us would be nothing in comparison. He's the reason we are all here together. We have to

111

defeat him or we are all done for."

"No way," Des said. "It's just some crank caller trying to mess with us."

Conall began to pace. "I think Amber is right. There's more to it. How'd he get my number in the first place? He said he got it from the *Horse of Darkness Comics Press*. But I should have known better. They would never give that information out. He also had my e-mail address. How did he get that? I bet he has tracked all of us through our social networking sites—things like that."

"Oh, come on," said Des, "it was just a crank call, but he was right, we don't need Amber."

Sadey got in his face. "We *do* need her. All four of us have to work together, but if we could get along without one person, it wouldn't be Amber." It was all Sadey could do to keep from saying it would be Des.

Conall said, "Whoever James Joyce is, he's not our friend, but Amber is. He is trying to control us. If he can't do that, he probably wants to split us up. Make us fight."

Des shook his head. It was obvious he disagreed. He did not see the caller as any kind of threat.

"He called me," said Conall, "and he called Sadey. He knows things about each one of us, even Amber. Besides that, how could he know about the battle we just had? That was minutes ago. There were no police involved, and no coverage by CNN. We didn't call to tell anyone else about it."

"Yes," added Sadey. "How did he know what was going on? He said to me on the phone that it was our 'vampire quarrel.' He called it a little 'test.' He knows Conall is a werewolf and that we just defeated a bunch of vampires."

"He is aware of all that," Amber interrupted. "Because he sent them!"

Sadey stopped. She knew Amber was right. The man on the phone was their archenemy—some kind of super villain.

Sadey went over and sat with Amber on Des' bed, giving her a long hug. She whispered, "I'm sorry for not believing you before, about being our Way-Giver."

Amber squeezed her tightly in return.

Des began to pace, but then he stopped. He looked at the other three and said, "I've been a fool. Those five vampires would never have returned on their own, and no way did they influence all those others to join with them. I don't know of a vampire leader powerful enough to send so many after us. Besides, they were from several different clans. That alone should have clued me." He paced again.

"James Joyce knows lots about us," said Conall. "We don't know squat about him. If he can influence fifty vampires to come after us, then we need more information—and fast!"

Sadey pulled out her cell phone and flipped it open. "I don't have GPS, but you guys do. Can that guy be tracking us, somehow, maybe through our phones?"

Des pulled his Smartphone out and began an Internet search.

Conall said, "It is one thing to tell our location, but how did James Joyce know I was into illustrating comics? I didn't even tell any of you guys. Also, how'd he know I was a werewolf? I didn't want to believe it myself, and I only told any of you recently. None of my family knows, and nobody else."

"I'd say he can definitely be tracking us through our Smartphones," Des said, raising his eyes from the little LCD screen.

Amber said, "For the first time, I'm glad I don't have one. I only get to borrow my mom's occasionally."

"Wait," Sadey said.

When the others looked at her, she held her finger to her lips, signing them to silence. She stood up and went to Des' dresser, pulling open different drawers until she held up a sock. She slipped her cell phone into it. Going to Conall, she signaled him to place his mobile in too. Next, she had Des turn his off, and add it to the two in the sock. She motioned for continued silence, and disappeared.

Sadey materialized in her basement and hid the sock in the no longer used oil furnace, inside a loose piece of duct pipe.

Back at Des' room, she signaled for the quiet to continue. She held up first one finger, mouthing the word one, then two fingers and mouthed two. After three, she raised both hands and nodded toward the ceiling.

The foursome instantly arrived at the old cemetery where Sadey had once placed Des and his parents under a tall grave marker as a warning. "Now we can talk," she said.

It was almost pitch black, although three of the four had amazing night vision. Amber, on the other hand, immediately tripped on a small headstone. "Ouch," she said, hopping on one foot.

When Amber quieted down, Sadey continued. "It only makes sense that James Joyce has bugged our bedrooms, and maybe other rooms too. I think he probably has little mini-cams, and he's been watching us. Who can say for how long? How else could he get that information about Conall?" She turned toward her shapeshifting friend. "Wouldn't he have to see you become a wolf? And observe you making drawings in order to find out you did that? How else could he have discovered it?"

"I don't know," Conall replied. "I guess you're right."

"Until we know more," Sadey said, "we have to stay away from places we usually go. That way, we can be certain he doesn't know what we're doing...or talking about. Otherwise, he will always be one step ahead of us."

"What about our phones?" Des asked.

Sadey explained, "I hid them in my basement. Until we know differently, I assume he can somehow follow us through them, probably by GPS. Maybe he even monitors our phone use. There was no point in us coming here, if we could be tracked by him."

Amber said, "He uses more than mechanical and electronic devices. He has a team of psychics in a special research lab. They do distant viewing, and future probability assessment. They predicted we would each develop as we have, and they sought us out and determined our locations. The man known as James Joyce wants to use us. If he can't do that, he will destroy our group, if possible. He can't afford for us to get stronger, and then oppose him."

"What should we do to fight back?" Sadey asked.

"I will focus in, and see if I can find his psychics," Amber said. "I know the lab is in Portland because I can feel its presence. Take my hand, Sadey, and when I squeeze, that means I've found them. We'll all go there, and with Sadey's help the three of you will follow me."

3: ARCHENEMY

SADEY WATCHED AMBER CLOSELY, EVEN as they held hands. Amber's eyes closed, and her breathing became shallow. Her facial muscles tightened—but then relaxed. Sadey realized their only hope was to locate and disrupt the psychics who tracked them. Could Amber trace their adversaries in reverse?

Conall began to walk among the nearby gravestones. He was pacing again. Sadey shot a look at him, but noticed he was beginning to turn. It was useless to try and interfere with that process. She glanced at Des, who had seated himself on a cemetery marker. His fangs showed clearly, as if their enemies were right in front of him. He seemed about to attack.

Some strong negative emotion surged in Sadey. Fear rose through her, but she fought it back. She was not afraid. It was a false emotion originating from outside her. She smiled. Their opponents were fearful, and attempting to send their own fears to affect her.

Sadey felt Amber retracing that path of dread, and knew her friend was getting closer as her hands squeezed, and became vice-like, Sadey brought the four of them together in her mind, and projected them along Amber's line of thought. She felt the nearness of her friends and a rush of momentum as they pushed through the psychics' projected panic, and were briefly drenched in it.

The four arrived as one, and found that the psychic laboratory was a stark place, composed of many small rooms, one apiece for each sensitive to operate from independently. There was also a control room, with audio and video equipment, and sensory monitors used to coordinate and direct the psychic operations.

The wolf was drawn to the control room, and Amber stood behind him in the hallway, watching with fascination as he slunk forward. Sadey turned her attention to the woman she saw through that window, and knew she must be the operations director. The woman's frantic eyes stared back.

Sadey appeared right behind the large woman. Seeing past her massive, shuddering form, and stringy hair, to the view screens and control boards that were lit up. Sadey observed Des in various monitors. He was the ultimate vampire, surging from room to room, yanking sensor pads from psychics and clamping his fangs on their necks.

It relieved and fascinated Sadey to see the level of control he had. Des did not go for the jugulars, but targeted instead some nerve cluster in their necks. He short-circuited those human electrical systems with surgical precision. The recipients just lay there, unable to rise nor mentally or psychically fight him.

Sadey said to the woman, "Don't move. It isn't you or these others we want. Where is the guy who set all this up? How can we locate him?"

"You will never find him," the woman said through trembling lips. "Leave now before he kills us all. You have no idea what you are dealing with here. This research is government funded. The rest—like when we remotely located and monitored you four—is just a sideline of his. This is completely top secret, and there are powerful forces supporting it."

Sadey realized there must be links in the lab to the man they sought. It would take some time, but—

Amber screamed, "Get us out NOW!"

Reflexively, Sadey gathered the four of them together in her mind to project them back into the cemetery. In the instant before she and her companions dematerialized, she felt the beginnings of a massive explosion. When they arrived in the graveyard, laboratory debris dropped around them, littering the ground. A moment longer, and they would have all been killed. Amber had saved them.

But, had they *all* made it safely away? Sadey looked about her. Despite the mess, it appeared her friends were unhurt, and simply badly shaken-up. It had been a narrow escape.

She said, "I'll be right back, guys. Stay here."

Sadey projected near the site of the psychic lab, but there was nothing left except a massive crater where the building had been. Thick dust hung in the air. Obviously, the people who had worked there had been destroyed. There would be no evidence to link with James Joyce. The crater was a dead end—literally.

Amber appeared a few feet away. "Come back. NOW." She moved closer and grabbed Sadey's hand.

Sadey realized that she fully trusted Amber's instincts.

They were back at the cemetery, but Sadey barely had time to see their two guy friends standing several feet away because Amber yelled. "Take us out of here, quick!"

Sadey prepared to teleport. Where should they go? Not to any of their houses....

"What's your hurry?" said a man's voice, not of their group.

Sadey recognized James Joyce's unique tone. As her mind scrambled to find a suitable destination where she and her friends could flee to, she said, "If you had never contacted us, we wouldn't know about you, or be seeking you."

He laughed and said, "Thanks for returning to the lab. I needed a way to find you. Just like I need worthy opponents. Life has become dull with always having everything my own way, and getting whatever I want."

Sadey said, "Deal with it, because we won't see you again."

She projected the foursome toward a new location, but she heard his last words.

"This is only the beginning...."

SADEY CHOSE TO TAKE REFUGE in her grandfather's cabin, with the words, "...only the beginning," echoing in her mind. The cabin was over on the Oregon coast, in Rockaway. It was a squarish, two-story affair with weathered T-111 siding that had never been painted. She thought of it because it was virtually burglarproof. Only her family knew how to remove the correct heavy plywood sheet identical to those that covered the doors and windows. An unnecessary effort currently, since they simply appeared inside.

Sadey looked around. It was just as she had remembered from her last visit, and at the present time of year, there were never any occupants in the cabin. Her companions quickly oriented themselves to their new environment, except for Amber, who couldn't see in the dark. She walked into a support pillar. "Ouch!"

Sadey saw Amber rubbing her forehead.

"You need a keeper," Des told her.

"Leave her alone," Sadey said, "If not for her, we'd all be vapor."

"We can't stay here," Amber said. The pain of her injury tainted her words. "Pick some random place." She rubbed her head again, "Ow, that really hurt—"

Amber added, "Take us outside the United States if you can, somewhere else, right now!"

NELSON, BRITISH COLUMBIA CAME INTO Sadey's mind. The picturesque town seemed to call to her. They appeared on the darkened streets, and Sadey wondered why she had been drawn there. She had vacationed in the region a few years previously with her family. That was before her little brother Ethan was born. It had been a peaceful trip, and the mid-summer weather had been perfect. Now it was cold. The frigid air chilled her almost instantly.

"Take us somewhere else," Amber said.

Even though they had just arrived in Canada, Sadey immediately projected her small group to Oaxaca, Mexico. It was a destination from another summer's vacation, also without Ethan.

SADEY CHOSE THE RODRIGUES HOUSEHOLD as their location to materialize—it was where her family had stayed one summer. Except, she projected the foursome into the enclosed backyard, not the house interior. The temperature in the more southerly latitude was much pleasanter than B.C. for that time of year. She took Amber's hand and led her safely through the dark. They didn't need her to crash into one of the papaya or citrus trees, and have an outburst.

Across the courtyard, the large rectangular home was of masonry construction. As with the surrounding houses, there was a twenty-foot-high wall enclosing the entire premises. The backyard was over one hundred feet deep, and contained a number of large fruit-bearing trees.

Sadey led her friends to the rear of the yard, to the laundry room nestled on the left side, and a one-bedroom apartment for a maid on the right. A stairway led above, to a small gardener's quarters, and a balcony where laundry was hung out to dry.

The Rodriguez family had a maid, but she was not a live-in servant, and she also performed whatever small amount of gardening they needed. Sadey made the others wait in the dark while she cautiously approached the maid's quarters. It sat vacant.

Moments later, the four of them were inside the single room that was meant for only a one person occupant.

"Where are we?" Conall asked.

Des chimed in, "Yeah. It smells funny here, wherever we are."

"Oaxaca, Mexico," Sadey said. "My parents and I stayed here with the Rodriquez family a few years ago, and I was sure this little apartment would be empty. There's even a toilet in the laundry room next door, so the maid wouldn't have to go in the house at night."

Amber said, "I don't know how long we will be able to stay here. So far, it feels okay. We need some backup locations, just in case. We should leave here before he locates us."

"We can go anywhere we want, right?" Des said. "I kind of like this idea, but why not the French Riviera?"

Conall added, "Or London...or Rome? We could go any place."

"Except for the crazy guy who's after us," Amber reminded. "As long as he's alive, we're in danger."

Sadey was noticeably quiet. She knew that hopping around the world would not be easy. Ideally, for safety, they had to know ahead of each projection where they would go. She needed to visualize their destination. Looking around at the tiny room they were crowded into, Sadey knew their hideout was far from ideal. It had a single bed, and they were uninvited guests. There wasn't enough money between them to afford a hotel room. Projecting to random street corners even in Oaxaca could become dangerous.

"What's wrong? Conall asked her.

Sadey slumped onto the old mattress. "I'm tired," she said. "We don't have enough sleeping space here, even if two of us move into the gardener's quarters. And I don't know where else we can go."

Silence filled the small room as Sadey's concerns sunk into her companions' awareness. She added, "Amber is right. We still don't know what we are up against. We need more information."

"The lab?" Conall asked.

Sadey gave a big sigh, "Nothing left. No equipment. No people."

"He killed all his own people?" Amber asked.

"Yes. The lady in charge tried to warn me just before...." Sadey paused. She realized James Joyce was a liar. "He didn't come after us for sport. He's afraid of us now. The last thing he wanted was to destroy his own laboratory, He needed to kill us. The remark about 'This is only the beginning,' was a bluff to throw us off. The loss of his lab will set him back. We have a chance now."

"Let's take this James Joyce guy out," Des suggested.

Conall said, "We don't know where he is."

"If only I'd thought to bring the lab supervisor," Sadey said.

Amber replied, "He would have followed us through her."

Sadey realized that was true, and said, "When I asked her how we could find him, she said we would never manage that, and to leave before he killed us all. 'You have no idea what you are dealing with here,' were her exact words. And there was something more… something she said about government funded research."

Sadey rubbed her temples, trying to remember. "Oh yes. She said that finding and monitoring us was just a sideline. The lab was top secret, and backed with big bucks…something like that."

"There is no choice," Des said. "We either find and take this guy out, or he will kill us the first chance he gets."

Amber moaned. "He is probing for us. He's almost got us. There was more than the one way he used to keep track of…On no…!

"Sadey. It's you. He's tracking us through you."

Conall asked, "How?"

"I have to figure that out," Amber said. "Go somewhere else, Sadey, quick. Leave us here, and then come back later. I will try and figure out how he's using you."

Sadey seized the first location that came into her mind and projected there alone.

4: TALL TOWER

*I*T WAS ALREADY TEN IN THE morning in Paris. Sadey gazed up in wonder at the Eiffel Tower in the distance. She had arrived at a long green expanse that continued clear to the imposing structure. A young woman was doing Tai chi, or something similar, off to Sadey's right. Pigeons walked about on the lengthy sidewalk, looking for food, their heads bobbing characteristically. One strutted and cooed, turning in circles.

No one seemed to have noticed her arrival. She began the long walk toward the famous tower. It was taller than any picture could ever convey. She had taken the virtual Online tour so many times she felt she had already visited. However, none of that had prepared her for the enormity of the actual structure.

As Sadey walked, she wondered what her friends were doing. Had Amber discovered the link connecting Sadey to their mysterious foe? How long should Sadey wait to rejoin her friends? Could she come back to the Eiffel Tower afterward, or did she need to keep changing destinations?

To heck with her fears. Sadey was in Paris, walking in the shadow of a world famous tourist attraction—almost in its shadow. She had better make the best of her opportunity. Sadey focused on an obscure spot beneath one of the four giant legs of the tower—

This is better, she thought, looking up at the corner of the tower from just beneath it. She had no money for a ticket to get to the first level...way up there!

I don't need a ticket, she thought, and picked a vacant spot on the observation platform, where she projected herself.

"Ah," she sighed with satisfaction, looking out across the Seine River at perhaps the most beautiful city in the world. Then she felt guilty. This is just what Des and Conall wanted to do. Visit London and Rome...the French Riviera. But if she had to keep going away from her friends, she might as well take in the sights. She smiled, thinking of them crowded onto the cramped bunk back in Oaxaca. Poor Amber, wedged between a vampire and a werewolf. She cringed with that image. Would the three be able to keep from killing one another in her absence?

Sadey was tempted to skip the elevator ride to the upper levels, and just project there. Then she noticed a security camera. Oops. She had better be more careful. The regular method would be fine.

Riding up in the elevator, she thought again of her friends. How long should she wait before returning to them? Would they be okay in her absence?

Twenty minutes later, Sadey gave in to guilt. She was also curious if Amber had figured out what it was that allowed someone to trace Sadey.

Focusing on a location just outside the one-bedroom apartment, Sadey projected there. She'd forgotten it was still nighttime in Oaxaca, where she overheard a passionate but muffled discussion going on within. The two guys were at it again. Why couldn't they learn to get along? When Sadey opened the door, silence filled the inner chamber.

"Did you figure it out?" she asked Amber.

"It's hard to concentrate with these two bickering," Amber said. "But I think so. Most likely, it's your watch, or maybe your ankle bracelet. I'm certain it is something you are wearing."

Those were both possibilities, Sadey thought.

"Drop them off in your bedroom and then come back. I'll see how I feel when you are near me then."

Sadey projected back home.

In her room, things looked out of place. Someone had gone through all her possessions. Did they take anything? As she removed her ankle bracelet, and then her watch, Sadey noted that nothing obvious was missing. She hid the two suspect items in the back of a drawer in her nightstand. Then an idea struck her.

Sadey projected to the guest bedroom, which was her Aunt Fern's room whenever she visited. Sadey never used the word "Aunt" to her face, and just referred to her as Fern. Since her aunt was ten years younger than Sadey's mother, she seemed and acted, at twenty-five, more like Sadey's older sister.

Sadey pushed the guest-room door closed and turned on the overhead light.

In the dresser she found brand new underwear that had never been worn. Her aunt was a shopaholic, luckily for Sadey. In the closet, she found clothes mostly worn only once. She picked out a classy skirt she knew would make her look older than she was. She added a chic top from the dresser, and rounded that out with two scarves, one bright, and the other conservative.

Sadey stripped out of her own clothes and dressed the way she thought her aunt would. When she looked in the mirror, she was stunned. The right clothes made a huge difference, and although she never carried one herself, she picked up a handbag that was lying on the bed. Looking inside, she found three hundred dollars in cash, a photo I.D. and two credit cards.

She'd hit the jackpot. Sadey wondered why her aunt had left those at their house. Was she a spy or something? Leading a double life? Fern visited almost every-other week, so Sadey wrote a hasty note of apology, begging her aunt to let her explain later.

Back to Oaxaca, she thought, and projected there again, outside the maid's quarters. She could not hear any big discussion like before between the two guys.

"What do you think?" she asked as she entered the room.

Conall said, "It hardly looks like you. A disguise might be good for all of us."

"You look *hot*," said Des.

Amber said, "I can't see you in the dark, but that seems to have done it. I don't get any warning feelings at all. To be safe though, we should probably leave here. Go someplace new."

"Any ideas," Sadey asked. "I'm running out of places. I've got some money now, but it gets expensive staying in hotels. We barely have enough for one night. Then there is food."

"We need a hideout," said Conall. "Somewhere we can stay for free that's secure, and no one else knows about."

"Let's find another temporary one for now," said Amber, "I'm starting to get a bad feeling about this location."

Sadey made an instant decision. "Okay, here we go—"

SADEY HAD SPOTTED A PARK only a long block away from the Eiffel Tower's main green belt. Many people hung out there, ate sack lunches, put their feet in the water features, or sat in shaded spots on the grass. It was an exceptionally inviting scene.

"Where are we?" Amber asked.

Sadey pointed at the tower behind her friend's back.

"Really?"

"How cool," Des whispered.

Conall glanced around. "This is more like it."

"We'll pretend to be regular tourists," Sadey explained. "We can talk and sightsee at the same time. It will make it even harder for someone to track us down."

Amber said, "What we really must do is overcome this James Joyce threat. I think we're finally a step ahead of him, but we want to get even farther and take control. No more catching up to do."

"The only way to do that," said Des, "is to discover who he is, and find out all we can. We need to get rid of him if possible."

"And we need a better place to hide out," said Sadey. "Roaming around Paris will be fun for a while, but we have to get practical. This is an expensive city."

She walked over and sat on a bench. The adrenaline from their narrow escape and frantic hide-and-go-seek adventures was wearing thin. She saw a couple of people dozing on blankets.

"I need a nap," she said, feeling exhausted. "Somebody watch over me, and two of you can go look around. We'll trade off." She took her scarves out of her purse and walked over to a shady location. Spreading them out like a makeshift blanket, she handed Amber her purse before lying down, and immediately fell asleep.

SOMETHING TICKLED SADEY'S NOSE. Worried about crawly things, she hurriedly wiped her face with her hand. That was how she discovered she was face down in the grass.

Where was she?

"We were starting to worry," said a familiar female voice.

Rolling over, Sadey said, "Amber?"

The sun had considerably lowered in the sky. She recognized the park after a moment, and gazed across at the Eiffel Tower. "Where are the guys?" she asked.

"They returned a couple of times," Amber said, "and then left to see more sights. I decided to stay with you."

The look of concern on Amber's face touched Sadey, and she moved one scarf beside her. Patting it. "Sit down."

Amber immediately plunked beside her. "I'm worried about our situation," Amber said. "I told you I am the Way-Giver, and that is the information that came to me. I don't know how I can help against James Joyce, though. This whole thing is awful scary. Blowing people up just so the four of us can't figure out who he is?"

"You saved us, Amber. Don't ever forget that. You've gone too long without sleep, and there's been too much stress to deal with. Take a nap, and I'll stay with you this time." Sadey took the scarf she was sitting on and handed it to Amber to be added with the other one so she could lie down.

Amber curled into a fetal position, but her breathing was too rapid. Sadey gently rubbed her friend's shoulders and upper back. "Just relax. Get some rest and you'll feel so much better."

In a few moments, Amber was asleep. That was when the guys returned, boisterous and full of life. Sadey gave them a look that would have caused a giant oak tree to wither and die, but it had a lesser, though desirable effect on the young males.

"You came to Paris to sleep?" Des whispered.

Sadey did not bother to answer him. Instead, she carefully took "her" purse off Amber's arm and removed some money. Handing Des two twenties, she whispered, "There should be some place around the Eiffel Tower to exchange these for French francs. Then find some nutritious food. Don't get junk...and bring what you two don't eat back for Amber and me."

The boys and the cash were gone in an instant.

"Figures," she whispered to herself.

It did not seem all that long before the guys returned, moving very rapidly. As they got closer, she saw the reason. They each carried two ice cream cones, and the ones they weren't licking were dribbling down their arms.

She stared at them in disbelief. "I thought I said...." But she was too exasperated to finish.

"You have to try this," Conall blurted.

Sadey decided after just one lick of the rapidly melting cone that Americans had probably done many things well, but when it came to ice cream, France had it all over the Yanks.

She ate Amber's cone too, whispering between licks, "We shouldn't wake her. She can have one after she gets up."

Both boys nodded expressively, but Sadey ignored their nonverbal, "Yeah-rights." She knew at that moment, sleep was a higher priority for Amber than food.

Twilight gradually descended, but there were so many lights on the Eiffel Tower that it was not as dark as it otherwise would have been. Sadey had no idea she'd slept so long, and without her watch she'd lost all track of the time.

Three teenage beauties paused a few feet away from Sadey and her friends. The girls talked rapidly to one another, and seemed not to be aware of the Americans.

Des, however, could not take his eyes off them. Sadey heard him whisper to Conall, "Burning hot, man...ooh-la-la."

Sadey appraised the girls. They were lovely, but they weren't French, because they spoke Spanish. One gave a side-glance at Sadey's male companions, but Sadey already knew the girls were interested in *her* guys. They would never have stopped so close by if they weren't. If they had actually been French, Sadey doubted they would have given even a passing glance to the boys.

She noted the girls were impeccably dressed and their makeup was flawless. They were definitely too sophisticated for a couple of guys from Independence, Oregon.

The three foreign girls began conversing again. This time, however, Sadey was certain they spoke Italian. Just then, Amber woke up. When Sadey looked down at her friend, she saw a look of alarm. Amber stared at the nearby trio of girls.

Sadey looked again at the female threesome. One of them, definitely the most beautiful, smiled broadly. Her vampire fangs were the largest Sadey had ever seen, and by then, she had seen more enamel sabers than she cared to remember. The sight sent goose bumps up her arms.

Amber's hand gripped Sadey's. "Get us out of here...please."

"Buon giorno," Des said to the striking she-vampire as she came closer.

Sadey did not know much Italian, but she thought he should have said "Ciao," instead. The gorgeous vampire moved with a silky elegance directly to him, ignoring Sadey and her other two companions.

The young woman moved her long dark hair back from her face, tucking it behind her ear, and the smile never left her parted lips. Sadey could not take her eyes off those pronounced fangs.

The dark beauty said to Des in strongly accented, but very good English, "You are Old-line...no?"

Although it was technically a question, she obviously knew the answer. Des nodded his head. "Si."

The other two girls moved with the grace of feline predators, and when they smiled, Sadey confirmed her suspicion—they were vampires as well.

The three young females gabbed with Des as if they were all old friends.

Amber's hand continued to grip Sadey, and she whispered, "I don't like this."

Sadey didn't either, but not because she thought her friends were in danger. She didn't like the attention the girl vampires gave Des, which aroused strong jealousy in her.

One of the vampires moved over to chat with Conall, and Sadey could hardly contain herself. It was bad enough, them hitting on Des. Making a move on Conall was totally over the top. Sadey felt a growl rising in her throat. Had she somehow learned that from here werewolf friend?

When Sadey felt she could not contain her anger any longer, she saw the dark beauty separate herself from Des and approach. As the girl neared, Sadey felt this was the most attractive female she had ever seen. Warm, dark eyes looked into Sadey's, and the smile that had been so wide diminished enough to reduce the impact of her fangs. How could anyone resist such a gorgeous girl? Especially, a vampire guy.

"I am Feliciana," she said, extending her hand. "I am from Italia."

Sadey found herself shaking the offered hand without hesitation. That came as a surprise to her. As courtesy dictated, she said, "I'm Sadey, and this is my friend Amber."

Feliciana's hand withdrew after the appropriate length of time, and she nodded to Amber, but returned her attention immediately to Sadey. "You know we are vampires?"

"Yes," Sadey replied, thinking how improbable this communication was if anyone overheard them.

Amber whispered, "I was wrong before, from fear. They are our allies...."

5: REVELATION

*F*ELICIA SAID TO SADEY, "IS TRUE. We are allies...if you wish. You are friend to Desiderio...nearly the last of the ancient ones, the Old-line. We are friends to him also, and therefore we are friends to you. You have fought with him, no?"

Sadey thought she could answer yes on two counts. However, she knew the reference was to helping Des fight off rival vampires, so she replied, "That is true."

"You have nothing to fear from us," Feliciana added. "You're under our protection while you remain in Paris...if you choose it."

Amber burst in, "Yes, please...we do."

Feliciana smiled down toward Amber in a kindly fashion. Amber had to squint hard to see her in the strange artificial light.

"Pleased to meet you, Amber," said the vampiress. "Thanking you for acceptance...of our humble offer. Do you have somewhere for the night...to stay?"

"No," Amber replied. "We don't know where to go."

"Then is settled," said Feliciana. "You guests...while in Paris."

Sadey could barely believe what she'd heard.

"Not so surprising," Feliciana said, apparently in response to the look on Sadey's face. "You are rare person. Friend to shape-shifter," she glanced over at Conall, "and to vampire," she nodded toward Des. "You bring peace where none was before."

Feliciana looked downward at Amber, "And you have saved all three. Des tells me this...."

Amber appeared too confused to respond.

Feliciana laughed. It was a short outburst that hinted at a much greater underlying mirth. "Almost, you were his first kill. You know this is correct, no?"

Amber nodded, and Sadey saw her friend's face flush with embarrassment.

Feliciana said, "I see why he wanted you." Her nostrils flared slightly. "We should go." She turned to Sadey, "Can you transport?"

Sadey did not know what Feliciana meant, and looked at her purse. Sadey probably had enough money to pay for cab fare.

Feliciana seemed to read her thoughts. "No. Like you transport your friends here. Des told me you do this. I would like to try it."

"Teleport?" Sadey asked.

"Yes, I think so. Can you do with us...also?"

Sadey didn't know if she could manage so many at once. "I'm not sure. Besides, I don't know where you live."

Feliciana said, "Not far. She looked at Amber, "You will follow me...." she reached out and lightly touched Amber's head. "Show Sadey with thoughts...the way, so she can bring me back."

"I'll try," Amber said uncertainly.

"You must meet my cousins," said Feliciana, motioning the other two over. "My cousin, Alita. She is from España...Spain."

Sadey noted the emphasis on the sound in the middle of the girl's name. Making it sound like Aleeeta.

"And this...my cousin from here in Paris, is Cherise." She pronounced that name as if it ended in a long Z-sound. No sooner had full introductions been made, than Feliciana looked at Amber but pointed to her own temple. "Follow now?"

"Uh-huh," Amber replied, and Feliciana whisked away, a streak in the night.

Amber closed her eyes in concentration, and reached out for Sadey. Would this work? Sadey felt Amber's focused thoughts following Feliciana. It was a dizzying pace to maintain, and Sadey was not certain her friend could hold the link.

"She's there," Amber reported. "She wants you to bring her to us. Can you feel where she is?"

Sadey was surprised that she could. "Yes." She held Feliciana's image, and pulled her back as an energy being.

Feliciana appeared right beside Sadey. She looked a little bit shaken up. "You did it! Can you go anywhere?"

"No, only familiar places. I don't really know how I do it. Amber can too, but just for herself."

Feliciana looked at Amber. "Show me."

Amber disappeared and then after a moment she came back. "Where did you go?" Cherise asked.

"To the place Feliciana went. It is the only place I know here."

Cherise laughed in surprise. "You went to my apartment?"

"Take us all," Feliciana said to Sadey.

In the blink of an eye, all seven young people appeared in a spacious Parisian apartment. "I'll show you where to sleep," Feliciana said. Sadey worried about doing such things publicly.

Amber and Sadey shared a large double bed, but it was not queen-sized. The coverlet was an ornate European affair the like of which Sadey had not seen before. They pulled it back and lay on the soft blanket underneath. Neither had bedclothes with them, but Sadey decided against returning home for more things until she was certain James Joyce, whoever he was, could not trap her there.

Cherise knocked lightly on the door and entered with a pile of silk pajamas, a pair for each of them.

"Merci," Sadey said.

"You are welcome. Sleep well."

After she had left, Sadey said to Amber as they changed into the elegant night things, "Do you realize what you did tonight?"

"I guess not."

"You remote viewed, just like the people in the psychic lab were doing to us. If we find the right information, I bet you can lead us to that creep who blew up the lab."

"James Joyce...? You really think I can?"

"Yes."

Amber said, "So do I. There is a feeling in me that I will soon know how to locate him. In fact...I think he lives in two places. Portland, and somewhere in the northeastern United States."

The bedchamber door swung silently open. Conall slunk inside in wolf form, with the Spanish vampire, Alita, draped across his back. She was scantily clothed and slowly stretched as she dismounted. With one last lingering motion, she ran her fingers through his long coat and slipped out of the room. "Gracias," she whispered.

What had they been doing? Sadey wondered.

Conall shifted back to human form as he ducked behind the door, hiding his nudity. "Be right back."

When he returned fully clothed, Des was with him. By then, Sadey was seething. Amber played the part of peacemaker. "We have a chance to find James Joyce and discover who he really is," she said.

Unable to let go of her anger, Sadey said, "If these she-vampires don't kill us in the night." Looking at Conall, she said, "You guys need to get some *rest*." She strongly overemphasized the word rest.

Des explained, "The three vampire cousins are highborn. Royalty in my world, and completely trustworthy. Our safety is important to them. Believe me, the midnight streets of Paris are a haven for some lowlifes you would not like to meet."

"How did they find us?" Sadey asked, still skeptical after Alita's entrance, riding on Conall.

"Just lucky," said Des. They caught my scent while Conall and I were exploring the Eiffel Tower. Then they were shadowing us. I should have caught on sooner, but I was in awe of all the sights."

"Where did you get money for *exploring* the Eiffel Tower?"

"Des is amazing," said Conall. "Girls couldn't do enough to help two stranded Americans. He used his hunting skills to get us where we wanted to go." Noticing the look on Sadey's face, he hastily added, "I meant, wherever in the tower—and no one got hurt."

"We have to focus on our objective," Amber reminded. "We can project there if you guys are ready, but we might want to change back into our regular clothes." She looked down at the silk pajamas she and Sadey wore.

Conall said, "I thought we were supposed to get some sleep."

"If Amber thinks the time is right to hunt for James Joyce, we better not put that off. Sleep will have to wait."

In an eye blink, street attire replaced Amber and Sadey's nightclothes. In that same second, Conall and Des had on the girls' silk pajamas for outerwear. A decidedly tight fit.

"Looking good, guys," Sadey quipped. She had Conall's under shorts on her index finger, twirling them around. Many of their clothes lay in piles on the bed.

"Knock it off," Conall growled, his face taking on a whiskery, pre-werewolf appearance.

Amber tried to keep her friends focused. "Please, Sadey."

In a wink, the guys looked more like American boys again.

Des said, "I don't think we should all go after James Joyce. You should send me in first and see what I can find out. I'll report back and when we know enough, then we'll all go."

Sadey wasn't sure that was a good idea.

"You should see him operate," said Conall. People are putty in his hands, and I don't mean just girls. Everybody."

"Amber will monitor my progress," said Des, "and Sadey can pull me out if necessary."

6: FORAY

SADEY DIDN'T LIKE THE IDEA of splitting up their group, but Des added, "It's much safer this way than all of us going in together. We can use Cherise's apartment for as long as we need to, and she and her cousins will guard you while I'm gone."

Sadey still didn't like the plan, but she could find no logical fault with it.

"He's in Portland," said Amber. "But he's not alone. He has the top floor in a newer apartment building. There is good surveillance there. I think the only way in, Des, is for Sadey to drop you inside the security camera perimeter. When you move, be fast, just a blur in the air. Stop, and then move quickly again. You can't just walk around in there. Oh, and he has guard dogs. Big, mean ones."

That was the only thing Amber said that caused a look of doubt on Des' face. He quickly shook that off, however. "I can do this."

As an afterthought, he asked, "What kind of dogs?"

Amber said, "A Doberman and two Rottweilers."

He tried to conceal his concern. "Piece of cake...send me in."

Amber looked at the others questioningly.

Sadey said, "Okay, but keep linked with me, Amber, so I can pull him out immediately if anything goes wrong."

"Make it so," Des said.

Amber's mind joined with Sadey's, who then saw the penthouse clearly. She followed Amber's lead to a vacant servant's quarters.

Then they mentally glided to a storage room with lots of cleaning supplies. "Back to the first," Sadey whispered softly to Amber in the Paris apartment.

She liked that initial location on the top floor James Joyce occupied because there was a communication hub for the butler. A servant could be contacted from anywhere on that level, and it was probably a two-way system. The viewing monitor was switched off, but likely worked. "Are you ready, Des?" she whispered.

"Yes."

She projected him into the servant's quarters, right in front of the communication monitor. It was a large screen, probably 32-inch. She saw Des look around the room and then, after a moment of study, he powered up the system. The screen lighted and software quickly initialized.

Multiple camera views came Online, and the screen filled with mini windows, each showing scenes from rooms on the top floor. There were halls, a roof panorama, and a street entrance scene.

"At last," said a voice that Sadey recognized as James Joyce. "What took you so long, Des...and where are your friends?"

"I'm alone," Des said, with no concern in his voice. "We've had a little falling out. I decided to take you up on your offer."

"Which offer was that?" asked the voice on the monitor.

Des said, "To work for you."

"That offer was for the three of you, not you alone."

"If I come and work for you, one or more of the others is sure to follow, but if you don't need more help, that's cool."

"Who would follow you?"

"Conall will. Sadey can be awful pushy. Wants everything her own way. And Amber—I think you were right—she doesn't know what she's doing. Once we get Conall, I'm sure Sadey will come around. She'll have to. Let *her* take orders for awhile." Des chuckled.

Sadey felt Amber mentally wince, but Sadey could see what Des was trying to do. If he convinced James Joyce he was defecting, he could gather information. Still, *was* she getting too bossy?

Sadey focused-in on the monitor. There was still no person visible in any of the screen's images, just bare rooms. There was a little flashing light under one picture, and a tiny sound icon with it. Supposedly, that was where the sound originated. However, the voice could be coming from anywhere. Des seemed barely to notice the monitor's video scenes.

At that same moment, back in Paris, Amber whispered to Sadey, "He's going to sic the dogs on Des. Better pull him out of there."

"No," Conall said, "send me in, too. I'll say I'm defecting. If the dogs come after us, I'll take them out, and I don't mean for a walk."

Sadey had to make a split-second decision. "We'll wait a minute. If we see the dogs getting near him, I'll send Conall in. If it looks like they might get Des, I'll pull him out, quick. But if we act too suddenly, we might mess up."

"Be ready," Amber cautioned.

As she had warned, the three large dogs appeared on a view screen. The guard dogs' approach was clear on the monitor as they moved down halls and through rooms. The Doberman was tall and lanky, and its movements were jittery. The mouth opened and closed compulsively. The two Rottweilers brought up the rear. They were lower to the ground and solidly built. Cautious and methodical in their approach, Sadey guessed they were the most dangerous.

"I want you to meet my pets, Des. Do you like dogs?"

"Not usually," said Des, "But I'm certain to like these. What are their names? Not something like Fido, I hope."

Sadey marveled at his calm.

James Joyce laughed. "I'll let them introduce themselves."

Sadey saw Des move unobtrusively, putting a thumb over a tiny video camera. Then he found a piece of scotch tape and some paper nearby on the table. With rapid movements the eye could barely follow, he made a more permanent cover for the mini-cam.

"Now," Amber urged, "send Conall to help him."

Sadey projected their companion to Portland, noting that he was already in wolf form when he "landed."

The Doberman came through the doorway looking battle-ready. It was clearly a well-trained attack dog. More agile even than it appeared, it leapt high for Des. When it was halfway to the vampire, the lean and agile guard dog noted that a wolf twice its size was also airborne, headed on a collision course.

The Doberman's alertness failed to counter the lightning moves of the wolf. Massive jaws seized the dog's neck and brought it to the floor with a thud. One mighty shake by the wolf, and the other's neck was broken.

Sadey gulped loudly back in Paris.

When the Rottweilers came through the entrance in Portland, they separated and moved methodically to flank the wolf. No sudden leaps for them.

Sadey saw Des nearly disappear, since he moved so rapidly, bounding off two walls and ending behind the Rottweilers. Well-trained as they were, they weren't used to the concept of two enemies from opposite locations. As they turned to meet the new threat, the werewolf immediately downed one. The second stayed focused on Des, its primary target. It barely saw movement before it was flipped upside down, and wolf fangs buried in its throat. In mere seconds, the battle had ended.

Back in Paris, Sadey found her breath was coming in gasps.

With a little effort, Des piled all three dogs on the table, which he had first shifted in front of the covered video camera. He motioned the wolf beside him, but out of view, and uncovered the lens. "Nice doggies," he said. "See how they stay so quietly, without moving?" After a long minute, he again covered the lens.

There was no scream of outrage, or uttered oath in response to the pile of dead dogs. Instead, with an overly controlled voice, the man known as James Joyce asked a simple question. "Are you familiar with the Assassino Vampiros?"

"Of course," Des replied. "They are legendary. As small children we hear stories about them. How they train from infancy to hunt and kill wayward vampires. The clan leaders have used them for centuries. No one has ever escaped them once the Assassino Vampiros are assigned to a kill mission."

"I knew you would be familiar. I bid you adieu. Oh, and Des...."

"Yes."

"Those were my favorite pets you so callously piled on the table. For that, I have instructed the Assassino Vampiros to take their time with you. They are masters of making their targeted victims suffer when they wish to do so."

"Only vampire clan leaders," Des said, "may command them. Yet, I can tell from your voice you are no vampire. Also, it is rare that more than one Assassino is used."

"For you," said the voice, "I have sent three. They are better than the best any vampire clan leader has ever commanded."

Sadey could tell from the look on Des' face this was *not* a good thing. She decided to pull him and Conall out of there.

Three figures appeared on the screen, repeating the same route the attack dogs had taken. Des lifted the surveillance equipment high in the air and swiftly smashed it—monitor and all. Then he said softly, mouthing rather than speaking the words, "We must face them *now*. Otherwise, they will pursue until they catch us."

From Paris, Sadey concluded Des and Conall could not handle three trained vampire assassins, but something in Des' statement made her delay their withdrawal.

In a whisper originating very near Sadey, in English strongly accented with Italian, Feliciana said, "We will help."

Sadey sensed that all three cousins were beside her.

Amber said, "It is the only way we can win. Project them to help Des and Conall now!"

Sadey linked to the three youthful she-vampires and teleported them to the penthouse floor of the Portland apartment building.

She said to Amber, "We need to cut off the power on that floor. Can you find the master switch?"

"Searching..."

"Hurry!"

"Getting closer...THERE!"

Sadey saw the source in her mind-link with Amber. She focused on the master breaker switch. No use causing it to turn off, she thought, someone might flip it back on. She dematerialized it, and then transported the entire switch to their room in Paris. "Lights out," she said.

Amber said, "The Assassino Vampiros were trained to kill other vampires, not werewolves. Conall is our secret weapon. They will not anticipate his strategy.

"I feel the assassins strongly," Amber quickly added. "Together, you and I can help disrupt them. They think like vampires, not like Conall or us."

"Nobody thinks like us," Sadey whispered as she focused with Amber on the drama unfolding thousands of miles away.

Sadey realized that in the 10,000-plus square foot apartment, the darkness might conceivably be a hindrance for James Joyce, but certainly was not for anyone of the other key participants. Although it was about three in the afternoon, sunlight did not reach the interior of the top floor. That was an apparent precaution from before, for security reasons, but it currently helped protect the vampire assassins.

Conall slunk away from Des and the female vampire cousins. Night forays were his domain.

"Let's stir them up," Sadey whispered to Amber. Focus on one, and I will project Conall behind him, just for an instant—then away." As Amber homed in on an enemy vampire, Sadey mentally connected to Conall, letting him know to act in a split second.

Sadey also found she could tune into the conversation between Des and the she-vampires. She asked him in thought if the three cousins were sensitive to daylight, and he said they were, but not too much. Sadey also wondered if the assassins were vulnerable to sunlight. He indicated that it was immediately deadly to them.

If we move fast, Sadey thought, we'll still catch James Joyce.

MENTAL TENSION FILLED THE DARKENED top-story of the building towering above the streets of Portland. At first, Sadey and Amber psychically positioned their point of view behind the three assassins. Those killers stayed in a triangular formation, with one in the front.

Occasional random forays by a single vampire assassin made the possibility of surprising them seem hopeless. In a surge of speed, an individual assassin would flit around a corner, or duck back behind the other two, so their movements were unpredictable.

Sadey worried about what Conall might be up to, so she and Amber shifted their attention until they located him. The werewolf moved steadily forward with a quiet gait. His direction was toward the vampire assassins, although Sadey had no idea how he knew their position.

"Their scent," Amber whispered to Sadey.

Sadey had begun to plot a rear attack of the assassins, thinking of using a brief projection of Conall. She would let him do his worst to one of them and then teleport him to safety.

"Not a good idea," Amber whispered. "Let him be the wolf that he is. His cunning is more ancient than the training of the vampires."

Nevertheless, Sadey did not trust the werewolf's instincts against killers taught their deadly craft from early childhood. She mentally thought to Conall, *'Be ready.'*

Sadey decided to time her action to follow immediately after one of the assassins made their random move. The lead vampire temporarily deployed behind the other two—a dozen feet to the rear. One of the others moved into the vacated point position, and a moment later, the initial assassin took up the other's empty spot.

At the same time, Sadey projected the werewolf behind the newly returned, flanking vampire. The wolf tore a chunk from the vampire's calf muscle and Sadey projected him away before the vampires could retaliate. The two unhurt assassins took defensive positions to guard their fallen comrade, and Sadey prepared to project Conall again.

Amber said, "No, Sadey. You will get him killed. Look at that vampire's injury. It is already healing. Since they know what you can do, they will have a counter move."

It looked to Sadey as though the injured vampire was not

healing very fast. He would be dramatically slowed. Still, she respected Amber's intuition. Sadey and Amber again focused their attention from just behind Conall. Every so often, they surged ahead of him to be sure there were no surprises, but Sadey worried when she was out of his sight.

She looked closely at the wolf's enormous head. His eyes were ultra alert, flitting occasionally to the side. His nostrils moved slightly as he analyzed every odor. Twenty feet from the end of a long passageway, he stopped. His nose actively sampled the air. When he resumed movement, each step was cautious. There was a dark look in his eyes, which no longer shifted attention from one place to another. He stared fixedly at the double doorway ahead.

Sadey wanted to shift her attention around the corner, but was fearful she would not be mentally with Conall when he needed her.

The wolf seemed certain that danger waited just around the corner, and Sadey believed he was probably correct. The urge to teleport him away was overwhelming.

"Don't," Amber warned.

Sadey anticipated the vampires would attack Conall when he passed through the doorway. It took her by surprise, therefore, when a single assassin came through the entrance at an angle, taking up a position to the left of the wolf. Conall took a slow, deliberate step toward this threat, his paw coming silently down. His eyes flitted between the vampire and the doorway, where it seemed a greater threat must be waiting to pounce.

The werewolf lowered into a crouch, his mouth open, fangs seeming to glint even in the near absence of light. A low growl thundered from deep in his throat. It appeared to Sadey as if he was on the verge of leaping at his foe.

She looked closely at the vampire. He was a truly dangerous opponent, but there was caution in his stance. He was wise enough not to underestimate the werewolf.

Conall's eyes glanced to the doorway, then back. He studied the assassin for a moment, and then focused briefly on the entrance. Returning his attention to the vampire, the wolf's muscles bunched. The vampire noticed, and pulled his body back a few inches, lowering, ready for the lunge.

The werewolf glanced again at the doorway. When his attention returned to the vampire, he rose slightly and retreated a half step. Then another, and another.

Sadey had mixed feelings. She was relieved, but disappointed.

They would have to face this enemy another day. She prepared to teleport her friends and allies back to Paris.

"Wait," Amber whispered.

As the werewolf turned to retrace his steps down the corridor, the vampire attacked. Conall was making haste, his tail tucked under his hind legs in the posture of fear and submission.

The assassin became a blur of motion Sadey could barely follow. She saw that the ends of his fingers had steel talons with razor-sharp tips. One arm swung downward to make a slashing blow across the wolf's back. Sadey was petrified and failed to act. She watched in horror as the talons made contact with the werewolf's shaggy coat.

That is when the wolf made his move. In a lightning motion, his rear end lowered, avoiding serious gashes. His head and neck arced around. Ignoring the clawed hands descending on him, he completed an unbelievable turn with his body and launched for the vampire's neck. Too late, the other saw his mistake. Deadly jaws clamped their mighty fangs on the vampire's throat. An awful snapping sound resulted.

The massive wolf stood there, waiting above the dead vampiro's body when the remaining two assassins entered the hallway.

Sadey only then understood how strategic Conall's every move had been. His retreat had not only fooled the assassin, but also lured him away from the entrance, making it more difficult for his two comrades to intervene.

The werewolf seemed not to notice as the other assassins neared. Instead, he stared fixedly at the still form on the floor.

"Leave some for us," Des's voice spoke from behind Conall at the opposite end of the corridor.

The assassins halted, taking in a new threat: Des and Feliciana.

Those two he-vampire assassins had separated, flanking the wolf, but now they moved closer together.

The werewolf growled loudly again. He moved forward in a low crouch toward the vampire he had earlier wounded. That enemy still favored his partially restored leg, and the wolf closed on him as if unaware of the third assassin.

The vampire limped backward a step, then another. The look in his eye said he knew the wolf would not stop until one of them was dead.

For no apparent reason, Sadey's werewolf friend acted as if he faced only one foe, and totally ignored the other.

Des and Feliciana were within ten feet of the wolf. The unhurt assassin clearly wanted to help his partner, but the odds were no longer in their favor. He glanced behind him to the doorway, where two more she-vampires, Alita and Cherise, entered. His chance to retreat had evaporated.

The werewolf launched into the air and took the injured vampire by the neck. The force of his attack carried them to the wall, and when the wolf stood, the assassin lay still, with his neck twisted.

The final member of the Assassino Vampiro trio made a seemingly futile assault on the she-vampires at the entranceway. He did not quite reach them. Des caught up with him in a burst of speed no human eye could follow. He bit the assassin's neck vertebrae as the two she-vampires each seized a clawed hand, and together they all tore away at him with their fangs.

His legs twitched in a death spasm. Sadey turned her focus away from that scene, back to the Paris apartment, and wished she'd done so even sooner. Through Amber, she was relayed Des' next words.

"Let Conall guard them," said Des. "We have to find our real enemy, James Joyce."

7: TRUE VILLAIN

*A*MBER JOINED SADEY IN PARIS by mentally returning to her body there, because she too could not stand the gore. She told Sadey that she had abandoned the werewolf when he seemed determined to "test" the carcasses to be certain they were dead. "I think he might tear their chests open and eat their hearts just to be sure they won't revive."

"How gross," Sadey whispered to herself. Then she said to Amber, "We should follow Des and the girls. What if they find the James Joyce guy?"

The two of them mentally returned to the Portland penthouse. At first, they followed Des and the three cousins. Amber, however, felt strongly they should project to an office located in the Northeast corner of the building. They found computers there with large monitors. The LCD screens showed security camera views throughout the building, with more extensive scenes than those in the servant's quarters. The monitors also dimly lit the room.

A door opened that likely accessed a private restroom. And a partially bald man entered the main office. He collected paperwork from one of the desks. Perhaps in his forties, he looked like a civil servant, not a criminal mastermind. Since the two girls were not there in physical form, he did not see them. This bothered Sadey. Apparently, James Joyce was not as omniscient as he had seemed.

He stuffed loose files, and sheets of paper into a briefcase, and began setting up what might be a bomb. Apparently, he intended to destroy all the evidence in the room, including the hard drives.

Sadey received communication from Amber indicating they

had to get Des there fast. Sadey found—during her mental search of the top floor—that Des and the three vampire cousins were still at a distance, separated from the office by a maze of rooms and hallways. Rather than try to contact them and give directions, she focused on their bodies, and dematerialized them. She brought them to the office with James Joyce, where they all appeared together.

Their archenemy tried to get away through the doorway, but Sadey had projected Des into the hall ahead of him.

Des backed the man into the office, where the fellow sat resignedly in a chair.

"Not your lucky day," Des said.

James Joyce nodded. "Apparently not. I knew the werewolf would be trouble. Now what?"

"We will look through these records you were about to destroy," replied Des. "We might go easier on you if you cooperate."

Sadey doubted that their enemy would be obliging. She also didn't think Des would be lenient.

"Oh, I'll cooperate," James Joyce said. "I know when I'm beat." Looking more relaxed than he should, he shifted position in his chair.

"It was fun while it lasted," he said. "When you took out my remote psychic unit, I knew it was all over...just a matter of time after that. Then you were flitting all over the place. Canada, Mexico...I don't know where after that."

Glancing at the pile of documents and records on a desk, he said, "Everything you need is right there. That's the stuff I was taking with me. It's what will keep me alive, and you with me. You won't know what to do with it, without my help." He leaned back, "It only ends here if we work together. They will kill us all, otherwise."

Amber whispered to Sadey back in Paris, "He's lying about working with us, but not about the records. Bring those here, now. But not the pile—the briefcase."

Sadey immediately teleported the vampire cousins to a spot between James Joyce and his attaché case. She dematerialized and brought the briefcase to Paris without anyone in the Portland room noticing. She also teleported Conall, still in his werewolf form back to Paris to help guard the records.

In the meantime, James Joyce was spilling his guts. Sadey thought that did not fit his character.

Amber whispered, "Something isn't right. Pull our guys out."

Sadey hesitated. It sounded like the little bald man was giving them good information, but something did feel vaguely wrong.

Plus, she wondered who had helped James Joyce seem to appear to them in the graveyard? Were there others closeby?

"NOW!" Amber screeched.

Sadey teleported all four vampires just as James Joyce clicked a pen that he'd carefully picked up from the table beside him.

*D*UST AND PAPERS FLOATED THROUGH the air in the room of the Paris apartment where Amber and Sadey waited.

Des coughed, and the three cousins patted his back.

The vampire cousins moved out of the way as Sadey and Amber rushed forward and tried to determine if he was all right. When Sadey turned to thank them for their help, they were gone. The leather briefcase had disappeared with them.

Conall had just taken human form, and said, "I guess we aren't the only ones who can teleport."

Feliciana's voice broadcast inside the room, "Thanks for your help. We hunted James Joyce for a decade. He got what he deserved. Use the apartment...how long you want. Lease is paid for a year. Ciao!" The three cousins shouted as one, "Bye, Des! We love you."

Silence filled the room—except for the sound of Des coughing. Sadey sat heavily in a chair. They had been so close to finding out everything. Now, all the leads were gone. Once again, a couple of her friends, plus the vampire cousins, had barely escaped alive.

"That wasn't the real James Joyce," Amber said. She held up a file of papers in the dust-laden air and smiled. "But we didn't lose everything with the briefcase."

Looking around suspiciously, Sadey wondered if she should project her friends and the few records they still had to a safer location? But where?

Unfortunately, Sadey was just too tired. She needed rest—

*W*HEN SADEY LIFTED HER WEARY head from the pillow the following morning, the room was dark. It took a moment before she realized she was not alone.

"You are awake...finally." It sounded like Feliciana's voice.

Trying to sit up, Sadey focused with her paranormal night vision, and saw all three female cousins lounging about the room on various pieces of furniture. A closer look revealed that Alita had draped her lithe form over the werewolf's back. He lay with his front paws stretched out before him. Beside one of his forelegs was the previously missing briefcase.

Sadey sat fully upright, staring at it.

"Is all there," said Feliciana. "Only couple papers missing. Little bit of editing we did, also. Removed private references—clan business, very private. No is importante to you. See?"

Only a close inspection of the contents would help Sadey determine if the Italian vampire told the truth.

Cherise spoke rapidly in French, which Sadey did not understand, but then said in accented English, as though she had read Sadey's mind, "We did not have to return the documents."

"I know," said Sadey. "Thank you for bringing them back."

The French vampire rose to her feet, retrieved the old briefcase, and brought it to Sadey.

"Merci," said Sadey. It was one of the few words she knew in that language. Unable to restrain herself, she undid the short leather strap from the antiquated buckle. She lifted the covering flap over the top of the old-fashioned attaché bag, because there were no zippers on the case, and certainly no Velcro tabs.

She pulled out a thick stack of file folders and documents from its interior that were bound together by a heavy-duty cord.

Alita rolled from the wolf's back and moved to the wall where she flicked-on a light switch. Amber and Des entered the chamber a moment afterward, as if on cue, and moved in Sadey's direction.

She blinked from the bright illumination, and then saw that a single, typewritten page topped the stack of paperwork beneath the rubber band. She paused—staring.

That moment seemed suspended in time. It was as if she'd journeyed to somewhere quite distant and important. The top paper was addressed to her, Conall and Des. Amber's name appeared on the second line, as if it were an afterthought.

Des and Amber gathered around her and she saw Conall shapeshifting back into human form. Sadey read aloud the undated typed page for everyone's benefit:

> *Dear Sadey, Conall and Des:*
> *(I suppose Amber also, if she's still alive)*
> *The fact you are reading this means you've prevailed—but only in the short run. You will not hear from me for a year or so, but when I return, rest assured, it will be to annihilate you.*

Surely, you did not believe the elimination of my puppet, the pathetic little bald guy you knew as James Joyce, was anything but a minor inconvenience to me. He was of no consequence, and had outlived his usefulness, anyway.

I am temporarily disappearing because the vampire leaders have taken too great an interest in my activities lately.

Best wishes to you three, and your little tag-along. Until our final encounter—

In place of a signature, there was a neatly drawn heart made from what appeared to be blood—now thoroughly dried and fully darkened. Sadey's hands shook slightly as she continued with effort to hold the sheet of paper.

"That is his biggest mistake," said Des, lowering his head and sniffing the dark symbol. "I will know him instantly, if we meet in the future."

Somehow, that was not a great comfort to Sadey.

"There will be plenty of time," said Feliciana, "to study those documents. For now, is good to—we be having some fun—NO?

Must see more of France, than only Paris."

FELICIANA'S WORDS HAD BARELY BEEN spoken when the entire group of seven rematerialized on a snow-free lower slope of Mount Blanc—appropriately dressed. They were in a simulated bobsled run, and their "sleds" were made of plastic, plus the runs were formed from undulating strips of concrete. In the background, a cloud formation clung to one side of the majestic white peak . Had Feliciana teleported them all? Sadey concluded she must have.

"Next, we go in ice cave," Feliciana whispered in Sadey's ear. "Come now, you and I ride together."

Most of the others were already gliding downhill, screaming with excitement. Sadey sat on her "bobsled" and felt Feliciana's arms wrap comfortingly around her. The Italian vampire said, "Have you been to Rome, yet?"

Sadey shook her head no. But of course, she'd always wanted to go there. In fact, for what seemed like forever, she'd longed to travel all around the world.

"We will visit them," Feliciana said, seemingly in reply to Sadey's thought as they slid downhill, careening around gentle corners of the snaking, paved path.

In spite of herself, Sadey screamed with delight. It had been far too long, weeks, it seemed, since she'd simply had fun.

In the wink of an eye, she appeared beside one bobsled after another, bumping them off-course, moving on to another just in time to hear the screeches of her friends and allies as their conveyances slid onto the grassy part of the hillside out of control.

Yes, she thought, having fun is good, and visiting Rome seemed like a particularly *great* idea...along with London... Amsterdam... Dublin...the Great Wall of China....

Back on her sled with Feliciana, she saw that Des and Conall were racing in her direction from behind, trying to catch up—those silly boys. Would they never learn?

With the written threat from the evil person behind James Joyce temporarily forgotten, Sadey said, "Ooh—wait!" because she realized she also wanted to see Stockholm, Berlin, Moscow, Buenos Aires, and....pretty much everywhere.

THE END

READER'S GUIDE

1. Who was your favorite character in *Werewolf Vampire Witch,* and why? (Just give your own opinion.)
2. What personal secret did Conall hide from others that caused him to miss the dance?
3. Why did Sadey feel she had to attend the Sadie Hawkins Dance, no matter what?
4. Who did Sadey really want to ask to the dance?
5. Could Des overcome his inherited need to kill, and if so, how?
6. What did Des do with his "juice" when he didn't drink it?
7. Were the four main characters able to maintain cooperation?
8. Is the book's character, James Joyce, a good guy or a villain?
9. Why do most characters go to Mt. Blanc by the story's end?
10. What happened to Des' parents? Did he still need their help, and if not, who helped him?
11. Did the main characters solve their major problem in Mexico, and what was that problem?
12. Who did Sadey, Conall, Des and Amber meet in Paris?
13. What powers or abilities did the four main characters have?
14. When did Des, Sadey, and Conall find the Way-Giver? Beginning, middle, or end of the book?
15. How did Sadey, Conall, and Des defeat a street filled with fierce vampires?
16. Who or what kept Amber from being killed in the graveyard?
17. If you could change places with one of the characters, which would you choose, and why?
18. Tell your favorite part in the story, and give your reasons.

To offer feedback on this book or these questions, go to **Contact** at:
www.eabundy.com

Author photo—at Saksaywaman, near Cusco, Peru

ABOUT THE AUTHOR

Oregon novelist E.A. Bundy has published titles in various genres (mostly YA & MG). This current story is another of his favorites. When he is not writing fanciful yarns, E.A. Bundy enjoys traveling, and in particular, exploring sites for even more upcoming novels. The photo above was taken during his visit to Peru where he was doing research for one of his *Matt & Mimi* series of time travel books.

He occasionally adds to his memoirs, including his exploits in the wilds of Borneo, and his discovery of H.G. Wells' time travel machine, which allowed him (so he tells us) to join with Hannibal in crossing the Alps. And, as if that were not enough, he purportedly sided with the Nabateans against Alexander the Great. E.A. Bundy's early training in magic came from the oracles of ancient Delphi—if we can believe him. And let's not forget to mention he purportedly wrestled 30-foot long crocodiles in Australia before going on an extended walk-about. (These accounts are undocumented—editor.)

For an alternate, perhaps more factual view of E.A. Bundy, we suggest you visit his website and decide for yourself what to believe:

www.eabundy.com

www.ingramcontent.com/pod-product-compliance
Lightning Source LLC
Chambersburg PA
CBHW071923220626
47052CB00002B/438